THE GIRL OUTSIDE

James Caine

CHAPTER ONE

The phone rang, startling Mandy Knox to the point where she almost rolled off the couch. Dead tired, Mandy got comfortable again and closed her eyes.

Today was not a good day. Whoever was calling could wait until she gave a shit.

After several rings, the call ended, and she could rejoice in her solitude again.

Was it James who called? she wondered briefly. *I should have picked up...or I could just call him.*

It was so *wrong* for her to be with him, but with what had happened at work today, all she could think about was screwing her bad day away. James could be a means to an end on that front, no matter how wrong it might be.

Callie opened the front door and stood over Mandy lying on the couch. "Hey, Mom," she said with a thin smile. "Bad day?"

"No, dear," Mandy said, sitting up. "*Grand day.*" She managed to smile at her daughter, trying to hold back from unloading her terrible day on her. Callie had heard about many of her bad days before. Mandy would tell her eventually, but until then, she would keep smiling and do anything it took to not drink her sorrows away.

The phone rang again. "I got it," Callie said, picking up the receiver. Her jovial face turned somber for a moment before she hung up.

"Who was it?" Mandy asked.

"Wrong number I think," she said. "They just hung up." Callie smiled and turned to the stairs. "Got study group with Jessica today. I'll be back before ten."

"What you studying?" she asked.

"Science," Callie said with a smile.

"Fun," Mandy said, rolling her eyes. "Need a ride?"

"I'm good. Looks like you need a break, Mom."

Mandy smiled back at her. "Well, have fun."

"Mom, we're studying."

Mandy laughed. "Well, have fun with that then."

Callie walked up the stairs towards her bedroom. Mandy couldn't believe her daughter would be graduating from high school in a little over a week, part of the graduating class of 1994. Her little girl was all grown up. When she turned eighteen a few months ago, it should have hit her then that her daughter was now an adult, but something about graduating high school made it real.

Callie had dreams of what she wanted to do after school. Juilliard for acting was the what she talked about the most. Maybe Mandy would get lucky, and she would stay in small town Cranston with her forever.

Somehow, she knew that wouldn't be Callie. She was destined for better things.

Mandy had had the same similar dreams of escaping Cranston when she was young. Instead, getting knocked up by her high school boyfriend brought her to where she was now—a waitress at a twenty-four-hour diner.

Scratch that. She had been a waitress at a twenty-four-hour diner. Her daughter had ruined her time brooding about what she would do next with life. Sure, it was just a waitressing job, and there would likely be others available at some point, even in a small town like Cranston. She had spent years catering to a rough group of people who came into her diner at all times of the night, most of them being truckers.

Now her daughter was a few more days away from finishing school and moving on with the next steps in her dream of being an actress. Mandy found herself almost jealous of her daughter's youth and determination. Did she know what her mother had to endure? Did she care that at one point, her Mandy had had dreams herself?

Mandy stood up from the couch, groaning at the aches in her body as she did. It wasn't too long ago that she'd had the world at her feet. Admittedly, she wasn't as smart as Callie. She might not have found her talent as young as her either.

Many men wanted her though. She always thought Callie looked almost as good as she did when she was her age. Had Mandy been single when she was her daughter's age, boys would have been lined up past Cranston and deep into Essex County.

Instead, she found herself over forty, a single mother and unemployed.

She truly had set the world on *fire*. If it weren't for Callie, nobody would even notice if she disappeared. Now, Callie would likely be leaving, and she would be by herself.

Her mouth salivated. She could almost taste a cold beer sliding down her throat. She could handle a light beer without going overboard with it, she thought. When Callie left, she could quickly run out and grab a small bottle of something harder even.

If she got desperate, she could even grab the old vodka bottle she kept in the attic. She hated the taste of it, but it would take the edge off.

She'd made a promise though, and she would keep it, this time.

Mandy looked at some of the pictures on her living room wall as if it were the first time she had seen them. The picture of her and Callie at Disneyland caught her eye. Callie was only a little girl. She was wrapped up in Mandy's arms, while Mikey Mouse gave her a high five. There was something magical about a little girl going to Disneyland around five years old. She was old enough to know that it wasn't the real Mickey Mouse under the costume, but still felt that magic as if it were.

Even when Callie was just five years old and her then husband lived with them, it felt like it was always Callie and her against the world. Even though her ex, Steve, took the photo of them, he was never really *there*. Mandy could barely remember any memories of the three of them together, besides the ones where the two of them fought.

She glanced at another picture of Callie on stage in costume as the Virgin Mary at the school Christmas play last year. Even though it was a high school production, it hadn't come off that way because of her daughters talent. The play itself was even on a local farmland, giving it a surreal experience. The drama teacher had said he had never seen a student with such potential that night.

Mandy scowled. Steve hadn't been there that night either. They had already been divorced for well over a year. She shouldn't have expected him to show. When he didn't show up after telling Callie he would be there, she'd felt heartbroken for her daughter. You wouldn't have known if it upset Callie though. She'd always been a good actress, and the show had to go on.

Mandy's expression changed as soon as she heard Callie's footsteps coming back down the stairs. She was dressed in a flowy yellow dress cut right below her knees. Her brown hair, tied up in a ponytail with a thick yellow scrunchie, bounced with each step she took.

Mandy smiled. What a woman her daughter had become overnight.

"I'll be back later tonight, Mom," Callie said, shrugging her heavy backpack up her shoulder.

Mandy nodded her head. "Just call if you'll be out past ten?" Callie nodded back in agreement.

Callie turned to leave, but Mandy grabbed her gently. "Hey, why don't we go out tomorrow. Girls' night out with your mom. Or is that lame?" It had been months since they spent quality time together. Mandy was always caught up with her own drama, and she'd somehow let her daughter's senior year at school slip past her. She regretted it, but then again, she regretted a lot of things.

Callie laughed. "Not lame, Mom. I can't though, Dad's picking me up early tomorrow."

"He is?"

"Yeah, he's taking me out to celebrate my graduation. He said he'll be busy when I actually graduate. You know him, he's driving a long haul, so he wanted to come by tomorrow instead. I told you, you don't remember?"

Mandy raised her arms. "Sorry. Must have slipped my mind."

"Bye," Callie said with a thin smile. A moment later, she left the home with a short wave to her mother.

Mandy took a deep breath. That small moment of satisfaction suddenly drained from her body.

Mandy looked back at the photos, focusing on the one of Callie on stage as the Virgin Mary. She sighed to herself and stared at the phone.

Don't call him. You always do this to yourself.

She picked up the phone anyway and dialed his number, and after a few rings, he answered. "Hello?"

"It's me," Mandy said, almost in a whisper.

"Oh, hey. Been thinking about me?"

Mandy sighed. She had, and she hated herself for doing so, but didn't answer him. "Did you call the house just now?"

He laughed. "You can just call me, you know. You don't have to play games, not with me."

"James, I'm serious."

"No, of course not. I know better."

"Callie picked up the phone. I—"

James interrupted her. "Let's see each other tonight."

Mandy smiled to herself but felt ashamed. "I can't. This was all a mistake." After the day she had at work, she wanted to see James, badly. That was all she could think about while lying on the coach with her sorrows. She'd fought the urge until now.

"I'm going to check in at the same motel as last time, in the same room," he said. She could almost see James' arrogant smile on the other side of the phone without even being there.

Mandy breathed slowly. "I can't do—"

"I'll see you soon." The sound of the phone disconnecting beeped in Mandy's ears until she hung up the receiver.

CHAPTER TWO

Mandy lay across the queen-sized motel bed, completely satisfied, breathing heavily and attempting to catch her breath. Her fingers clutched the sheets, grounding her back to the moment.

James' hand caressed the side of her body, until he clamped on to her waist. "I knew you would come." He smiled at Mandy devilishly, as if ready for round three. "I just wasn't sure how many times."

"Shut up," Mandy said, striking him with a pillow.

James rubbed her outer thigh, lying next to her. She could still feel the intensity of the heat from his body as if he were still on top of her. "I'm getting tired of meeting you at motel rooms. We could go to my parents' place. It's been empty for years, and I use it when I need a nice getaway."

Mandy's body suddenly got tense. "Don't even joke about that. What if he showed up there?"

"Steve?" James laughed. "He never would. Besides the property is in my name, not his. You remember the wooded area behind the cabin? I love it there. I could get lost for hours and just feel part of nature."

"You know more than anybody the type of man Steve is. He would kill you if he found out."

"I can handle him," he said, assuring himself.

Mandy knew that wasn't true. Steve Knox had a reputation as a tough guy in town. He would willingly take on anybody who challenged his reputation. Now that Steve was forty-six, he wasn't fighting as much as he did years prior, but he was still dangerous.

"That's why this is a mistake," Mandy said out loud, but mostly to herself. "We can't sneak around Cranston like this. Someone will find out, then he finds out. I shouldn't have come."

James removed his hand from Mandy, and lay back on his pillow, staring at the ceiling. "You did, and you will again and again." Mandy turned her body away from him. "Why did you even come here then?" James asked with a sharp tone. "You know how I feel about you. You know how I've felt about you my whole life. You're not the only one with feelings, you know."

Mandy turned towards James, laying her hand on his bare chest. "I know how you feel about me." She caressed the hairs on his chest while thinking about what to say next. "I just...had a bad day. I'm sorry."

"What happened?"

Mandy sighed. "Dean."

"Your boss?"

"The manager, yeah. He fired me today."

James sat up in the bed. "Why?"

"Stupid stuff. I don't want to get into it right now." Mandy put her hand to her head. She was worried what James would do if she told him.

"You were waitressing there for what, eight years?"

"Almost ten," Mandy corrected.

James breathed deep. "What a weasel. This is the same one who hit on Callie that one time?"

"Yeah. Callie picked me up from the diner one day. He made some slimeball comment about how good she would look in a waitress uniform. He said she would be even better looking than her mother. Ugh. I would have killed him if he touched her." James looked at her with an arched eyebrow. "I would have! That was when she was only sixteen." Mandy thought about Callie someday moving away from Cranston. "I'd kill anybody who touched her like that."

"Now that she's eighteen, you will have to get used to men noticing her." Mandy looked at him coldly. "What? It's true," James said. "It's not her fault. It's yours really. She looks just like you when you were young. Blame your genes."

"Doesn't matter," Mandy said. "She'll be leaving soon enough. A town like Cranston is too small for a girl like Callie. She has her whole life ahead of her."

"You do too," James said, striking Mandy back with a pillow. "You deserve to share that life with someone who will treat you right. I meant what I said before. I'd give up my job. I'd stop travelling everywhere and stay here with you."

Mandy laughed. "What would all your young girlfriends think?" James rolled his eyes. Mandy sighed. "I tried marriage. I already told you I won't try it again, especially with you." She noticed the motel clock on the wall read nine forty-five. "I should go back home. Callie will be back soon."

"Until next time," James said with a confident smile.

Mandy left the motel, taking her time saying goodbye to James. When she got to the parking lot, she felt odd. It was as if someone was watching her. She looked out into the parking lot and across the street at an empty office building, but saw no one.

Mandy knew what she was doing was wrong. Her feeling this way could be just her own conscience playing on her guilt.

She quickly got into her beat-up Volkswagen and turned the key. The lights flickered, and it felt like her car was about to die, again, in the middle of the parking lot. She turned the car key again, and thankfully, it started.

She made it home almost twenty minutes past ten. Mandy parked in her driveway, and entered her home through the side entrance. When she opened the door, she called out for Callie, but she didn't reply. Mandy put her shoes in the closet and looked around the dark home.

She walked up the stairs and noticed a light coming from underneath Callie's bedroom door. She walked up to her daughters' room, raising a hand, but didn't knock. Instead, she slowly lowered her hand and walked slowly to her room, closing the door silently behind her.

Mandy slipped into her bedsheets, not changing out of her clothes. All she could think about was how much she hated her boss, how much she hated herself for going to James, and how much she would miss Callie when she ultimately left her.

The small amount of satisfaction that James provided her leaked from her body, leaving her with all the remorseful thoughts and memories.

Mandy got up from bed and opened her closet door. She stood on her tiptoes, reaching into the upper closet under some old towels, until she could feel her fingers wrap around the grip. She pulled out the handgun and slipped out the clip, like how her husband had showed her when they were married.

The weight of the gun in her hand made her feel comfort. Sometimes, it was the only thing that made her feel this way, besides being drunk, but it had been over a year since she had a drop.

She slipped the gun back under the towels in the closet and got back into her bed, starring at the ceiling until she somehow managed to drift asleep.

CHAPTER THREE

Mandy woke up to the sunlight blinding her through her open window. She was usually up before five in the morning, getting ready for work, and on the rare day off she had, she still enjoyed being up and ready for her day.

Today was a different story.

She looked at her clock and saw it was already past eighth-thirty. After showering and changing into comfortable clothes, she went downstairs and into her kitchen. She reached into a high cabinet, sorting through the items until she grabbed the bag of instant coffee.

She wasn't sure how long it had been up there for. She had always had her coffee at the diner at work. Things had changed now. On a positive note, instant coffee took a while to spoil, so she assumed she was safe drinking it.

After boiling the water and adding the instant coffee, she took her first sip and felt different immediately. She spat out the dirty water in her sink and dumped her fresh brew down the drain as well. With enthusiasm, she tossed the bag of instant coffee into the garbage.

Some things aren't worth keeping.

Mandy noticed yesterday's paper at her kitchen table. Unhappy about the lack of coffee beside her, she opened the paper to the classified section. She needed to start looking for what she would do next with her life.

Experience an asset. Post-secondary education required.

Reading the job ads made her feel sick already. How could

she find a job in her forties with little work experience besides giving people coffee? She couldn't even do that for herself now.

As she skimmed the paper, one ad caught her attention. *Female Phone Operator Needed. A female with a nice voice is needed to work with a passionate clientele who enjoy meeting new women over the phone. No experience needed.*

Mandy flopped the paper on the table. *Great. I have a great future as a phone sex operator.*

The phone rang, and Mandy picked up the receiver. "Hello?" She waited a moment for someone to respond, but it was silent. "Hello?" She waited a bit longer, and when nobody said anything, hung up the phone.

Mandy stood up and walked into her living room, flopping onto her couch. She turned on the television. She flicked through a few channels until she settled on *The Jerry Springer Show*. She had always heard about the delightful guilt people felt while watching daytime television, and after ten minutes, she understood why.

For a moment, she worried that Callie would come down the stairs and catch her mom being lazy on the couch in her jogging pants. Luckily, at this time she would be already at school.

Is this what I've become? she asked herself. Yesterday was her day to sulk on the couch. Today she had a plan, sort of. Stay active. Do things around the house. Get groceries. Do anything but sit on the couch all day and eat bad food.

Do anything but call James again.

Yesterday, her boss Dean had told her she could pick up her last check today at the diner. She worried about showing up at the diner after the scene she'd made yesterday. When she needed the money, she would pick up her last check.

Of course, she needed the money right away, but she didn't want to admit it.

She thought about asking Callie to go out today after school to celebrate her graduating. Why did Mandy give up so quickly when Callie said she was going out with Steve? Mandy didn't even bother to ask for a different time to do something with her.

Is that how sensitive I've become?

Fuck Steve, and Dean.

Mandy turned off the television. She changed into normal clothes and planned to go to the diner after all. She knew it would be nice to see her coworkers again. They were on her side anyway but wouldn't dare speak up to Dean like she had the day before.

Mandy walked up the stairs, slowing down when she went by Callie's room. She opened the bedroom door and was almost caught off guard by how dirty it was for a change. Mandy had never had to tell her daughter to clean her room. Callie's room was always pristine to the point that it made Mandy feel guilty for how badly she kept up with the rest of the house. Usually, when the house was in great shape, it was because of Callie.

A lump of dirty clothes was on top of the corner of the bed. A bra was hanging over the side, teetering on falling. Her desk was also filled with items that were typically on the shelf beside it. Mandy looked and noticed the bedroom light was still on.

Did Callie forget to turn off her light? Maybe she left for school earlier than normal to study more. What was her test on again?

For a moment, she could feel her heart beat faster, but realized she was being dumb. Callie was already at school. How many times had Mandy come home later than expected and Callie had told her how worried she was? It was normal to worry.

Mandy turned off the bedroom light, closing the door behind her gently. When Callie came home from school, Mandy would take her daughter out for much needed quality time together and wouldn't take no for an answer this time.

After, she did exactly what she'd planned after changing into jeans and a T-shirt—kept busy. She ran her errands, cleaned out the fridge, and gave the floors a good cleaning. Mandy smiled to herself, thinking Callie would be surprised at how clean everything looked when she came home from school.

She saved the hardest task for last though.

She drove to the diner practicing how she would respond to made-up questions she assumed her coworkers would ask. Every time she could see them encouraging her for standing up to Dean and not taking his shit. She made sure to go when Dean wasn't typically at the diner.

She parked in the Anytime Diner's parking lot. It was filled with more cars than usual. She knew the day staff would have a difficult time keeping up with all the customers without her and worried about them. Keeping up with a customer's needs had a direct impact on tips they gave you. If they were now short-staffed and without their lead waitress, how well could they do?

Mandy had trained the new girl, Karen, just last week. Mandy made sure to bolster Karen's confidence with praise for the small things she could do well, but the truth was she was terrible. She had dropped several plates when bringing food to a table, driving Dean furious at the loss of income from having to make a new order of food.

Mandy walked through the doors. She spotted her work bestie, Noelle, taking down an order from a customer in the back of the diner. Karen was bringing a plate full of food to a table, and Mandy smiled, noticing how wobbly her wrist looked while trying to balance the food. This time, Karen managed to successfully put the food on the table instead of the floor.

To her surprise though, nobody noticed Mandy. The customers she had served for years kept eating. Her coworkers continued to work as if she weren't there. Mandy breathed deeply. Usually, she would enter the diner and head right to the back office to get ready for her shift, but today, she felt out of place, not knowing what to do.

Noelle finally stared at her, with a solemn look. If Mandy could read minds, she would hear her coworkers thinking, '*what the fuck are you doing here?*'

Mandy sat at the counter and waited for Noelle or Karen to come to her. She thought about just going through the kitchen to the back office, grabbing her check, and storming out, but decided on a more subtle approach today.

"What are you doing here?" The mistakenly old and screechy voice could only have been Dean. His shirt, which barely contained his belly, had large stain on it.

Mandy was annoyed at his question, since it was him who'd said to come. "You said I could pick up my check today," Mandy answered defiantly.

"You said a lot of things yesterday too," he said with a sneer.

Mandy lowered her head. "I thought you would be gone at this time. You usually are."

Dean waved his hand around the room. "We're busier than usual. I had to come in."

Mandy sighed. "Can you just grab my check?"

Dean smiled. "You wait here!" he said sternly. "If you cause another scene like yesterday, I'll just call the cops."

Mandy bit her lip before bad words came out. Cops? She would welcome them. Dean was in the wrong, no matter how much he tried to change the story.

Dean left towards the kitchen, and Noelle and Karen swarmed around Mandy like vultures.

"Are you okay?" Noelle asked.

Karen laughed. "I can't believe you're here right now!"

"I need my money," Mandy said. She gave Karen with a sympathetic look. "I could really use some good coffee too."

Karen nodded her head and grabbed a mug.

"You don't have to act tough," Noelle said. "Yesterday was bad."

"What can I say?" Mandy replied. "My life's a complete mess, and I'm too old to change it. Coffee makes everything better though," Mandy said as Karen put a mug beside her, spilling some coffee on the counter.

Dean moved slowly back into the dining area, tossing an envelope at Mandy. The envelope landed in the small puddle of spilt coffee, soaking up its brown juices. "Now, leave," he said with a stern voice.

There was something more than just his tone that bothered Mandy. He was no longer her boss, but was still telling her what to do. Not anymore! Mandy took a dollar bill out of her purse and put it gently on the counter, sliding it towards Karen.

"Paying customer," Mandy said, staring at Dean harshly.

She raised her mug, but Dean's thick fingers wrapped around the mug, easily taking it from Mandy.

"Keep your welfare money," Dean said, pouring the coffee in the sink behind him. "Do I need to call the cops this time?"

Mandy stood. "No, but I can call my lawyer."

Dean laughed. "The only one you know is your divorce lawyer. Now, get your skinny ass out of my diner and don't come back."

She bit her lower lip, knowing better than to make another scene like yesterday. Noelle was standing behind Dean, shaking her head, pleading with Mandy to let it be. Karen was watching the exchange with the same intensity Mandy had when watching *Jerry Springer* that morning.

Dean maintained his smug shit eating grin, waiting for Mandy to explode. He was the one who touched her inappropriately yesterday. He had walked sideways as Mandy passed by him carrying food for a table when his hand *accidently* brushed past her breast. He had done this to her in the past, but yesterday she had had enough. He enjoyed playing games with her, and getting away with it, until she stood up for herself yesterday.

Mandy grabbed her dollar, stuffing it into her purse. She looked at Dean harshly. "And stop calling my house! I'm done playing games with you! I'll call my lawyer." Dean laughed loudly as Mandy left.

She stormed back into her Volkswagen, driving back to her house much faster than legally allowed.

Just wait till I tell Callie what happened with Dean this time, she thought.

She sat in her car, in the driveway beside her home, and noticed the time on her car radio clock. School had ended almost thirty minutes ago. Mandy opened the side door into her home from the driveway. She planned on telling Callie everything that had been happening, perhaps over dinner somewhere.

She thought of James for a moment. Well, she wouldn't share everything.

Mandy walked inside her home and heard the phone ringing again. She tossed her shoes into the closet and made her way to the kitchen phone, but it stopped ringing before she could pick up. Mandy waited for the answering machine to turn on, but it didn't. Whoever was calling didn't bother to leave a message.

"Callie!" she yelled, but no one answered. "Callie! You here?"

The phone rang again, and Mandy picked up the receiver. "Hello?" The person who called said nothing. "Whoever this is, stop! Dean! Stop it, now!" She heard a woman laugh, then the call ended.

Mandy hung up the phone. She turned the phone over on the counter and disconnected the wire. If whoever was calling wanted to freak Mandy out, it was working.

"Callie! Are you home?"

CHAPTER FOUR

She still wasn't home.

Mandy breathed deeply, trying to collect herself.

Last night, she hadn't checked on Callie before going to bed. Her daughter's bedroom door had been closed, with the light left on. This morning, she woke up and Callie's bedroom light had still been on. Now, she wasn't back from school.

Mandy had a rotten feeling in her stomach. She picked up the kitchen phone to call the school, but realized she didn't know the number. Searching the drawers around her, she finally found the Yellow Pages. She opened the telephone directory book, sifting through the thin, flimsy pages.

She's probably doing some drama thing.

There was always an end of the year play, but Callie hadn't mentioned what part she had. After her lead role in *Romeo and Juliet* last year and playing the Virgin Mary in this year's Christmas play, maybe she was upset about not getting a huge part and didn't tell Mandy. She could still be studying.

When was her test again?

What do I say when I call the school? Mandy closed the telephone book. *Hey, where's my daughter?*

The school was only a few minutes away. Was she really going to embarrass herself instead of going to the school and just finding Callie?

Mandy opened the closet near the side door, tirelessly searching for her misplaced shoes. She ran to her Volkswagen parked in the driveway, thinking how silly she must look to her neighbors if they were watching.

It only took a few minutes for her to get to the school and park in the nearly empty lot. It was Friday afternoon, so of course all the students would run out of here, but not Callie.

She entered the school doors through the front lobby. Pictures of the senior students were spread across the main hallway walls, with something written beneath them. She noticed a pretty blonde girl on the wall, instantly knowing it was Callie's friend, Jessica. They were in drama together too. She remembered listening to the girls study their lines for the school play last semester. Mandy stopped to read the message beneath Jessica's graduation portrait.

"If you want it bad enough, you can have almost anything."

The words put a smile on Mandy's face, thinking of her daughter. She looked down the hall at the other student portraits. All of them wearing their dark cap and gown. She tried to spot Callie's, but it seemed they weren't in alphabetical order.

Drama class was taught in the auditorium, which Mandy remembered her daughter telling her. She spotted the doors to the auditorium from the main hallway and quickly made her way there, opening the doors to the sound of silence and a dark room. Mandy's smile dropped. The heavy doors closed behind her, making the large room even darker.

Mandy peered out into the empty theatre chairs and finally at the bare stage. There were no props or set pieces in the room. It looked as if she'd entered the theatre of a shuttered production.

"Can I help you?" A short man lifted the stage curtain, revealing himself. She instantly recognized the young drama teacher. "Ms. Knox?" It appeared he could recognize her as well.

"Yes! Hey, Mr. Peterson, right? I was looking for Callie, but she must be in her study group or something." Mr. Peterson hopped off the stage and walked up the aisle towards her. The teacher was young, and Mandy remembered him for always wearing bright clothing, which Callie had said his students made fun of him for. Today, he didn't disappoint. His ensemble included bright pink pants, a blue shirt tucked in, and a grey bowtie.

"Study group?" he said with a raised eyebrow.

"Well, I assume she's still studying with her friend. She mentioned she had a big final test coming up. For some reason though, I figured she would be here, since she lives in this room." Mr. Peterson laughed. "When is the final play by the way?" Mandy asked, looking at the empty room.

"Please, call me Rand. It's the end of the school year now. I go back to being a regular human being for the summer months. But we're all done for the year."

Mandy tried to hold back her surprise. "There's always an end of the year play though, right?"

"Of course!" Rand said.

"Why didn't Callie tell me?" Mandy tried to hold back her anger at the thought of Callie being on stage while her father watched from the crowd. He had probably taken her out for a congratulatory dinner after the show as well, while her mother was in the dark about it all.

Rand furrowed his eyebrows. "Ms. Knox, Callie wasn't in the play." This time, Mandy couldn't hold the shocked expression from her face. "She hasn't been involved in drama all semester. I tried... I wanted her for a main part, but not the lead. Some of the girls get jealous if you give the lead twice to the same girl, not that she didn't deserve it. She is by far the best student I have ever had."

"What?" Mandy asked on a breath.

"I couldn't give her the lead," Rand said. "Maybe she was upset by that, I don't know. She dropped out of drama class entirely. She didn't want anything to do with drama the last few months. I tried to talk her into coming back, but she refused. She wouldn't tell me why."

Mandy stood in the nearly empty room, trying to listen to the drama teacher, but she was wondering what the hell was going on. She wasn't able to speak momentarily.

"I know things haven't been well at home," Rand said with a genuine look of concern on his face.

Mandy finally found her voice. "She told you?"

"Not exactly," he answered. "This room may be large, but our voices carry. I know she's been having a tough semester. I tried everything I could to get her to come back, though."

"Why didn't you call me? Tell me?" Mandy asked with a hint of anger. Rand looked at her confused. He was attempting to say something, stumbling over his words, when Mandy cut him off. "Where's my daughter?'

"*Study group*?" Rand said with a thin smile, raising his hands.

Mandy cooled herself and asked who taught science to Callie. Rand said he wasn't sure which science teacher had Callie this semester but said they only had two at Cranston High.

"Mr. Greyson and Ms. Apple. Yes, she's a science teacher, and her name is Ms. Apple." He smiled to himself. "I can bring you to their classrooms if you like?" Rand said with a placating smile.

"Thank you, Mr. Peterson."

Rand guided her down several halls, stopping finally at a closed door. He knocked a few times, but when they heard nothing coming from the other side, he turned to Mandy. "Ms. Apple must have left for the weekend already. She's got this nice vacation home on an acreage nearby. I don't blame her. Mr. Greyson is upstairs." Mandy nodded her head, annoyed with the backstory and wanting to just see her daughter. The school wasn't large, but time seemed to move in slow motion before they finally reached the science teacher's classroom.

Rand entered the science room, while Mandy slowly followed, hoping to find Callie's beautiful smile in the room immediately. The room was empty except for the three of them.

"Hey, Mr. Greyson," Rand said to the science teacher. "Have you seen Callie Knox today?"

The science teacher brushed his medium cut brown hair to the side, revealing his bright blue eyes. "That's a good one," he said with a laugh. The teacher looked up and saw Mandy concerned face.

Mr. Greyson's eyes widened. He reached out a hand to Mandy. "Oh, sorry. You must be—"

"Callie's mother, yes." They shook hands for the first time, and she noticed Mr. Greyson's grip was soft. Her ex-husband, Steve, hated soft, limp handshakes. It told you everything you needed to know about a man, he would say. Steve might have been manly, but he hadn't been a good husband. "Maybe she's in the library?" Greyson said to Mandy. She looked at Rand for a reassuring nod. "Isn't that where the kids study sometimes?" he continued. He suddenly looked confused. "Study for what though?"

"She has her final test for science coming up, right?" Mandy pointed out.

The teachers shared a look between them.

Mr. Greyson looked at her with concern. "This is the final week of school. All tests are done."

"Oh," Mandy said with a blank expression.

"Not that Callie came for the test," Mr. Greyson said. "She skipped that too."

"What do you mean?"

"I mean she barely shows up," the science teacher explained.

Mandy covered her forehead, applying pressure with her hand. "I think I need to speak to the principal. He's still here, right?

"*She*, Ms. Knox," Mr. Greyson said. "I think you're thinking of Mr. Jeffers. He retired last year." Mr. Greyson looked back at Rand with a smile. "Ms. Blacksmith is our principal now."

"Would you like me to bring you to her office, Ms. Knox?" Rand offered.

Mandy let out a sigh and left the classroom. She knew where the principal's office was. She had been there several times to speak to Mr. Jeffers and the guidance counsellor about Callie making it to the principal's honor roll the past few years.

Mandy took a deep breath before entering Ms. Blacksmith's office. When she finally managed to open the door, a receptionist greeted her.

"Hi, I'm looking for Ms. Blacksmith," Mandy said managing a smile.

"Do you have an appointment?" the woman asked.

"No, I don't. I—"

"Ms. Blacksmith has one last appointment today."

Mandy let out a sigh. "Yes, I understand it's the weekend. My name is Mandy Knox. I…I'm looking for my daughter."

A lean woman came from out of the back office. "That's okay, Clara. I can fit Ms. Knox in before my next appointment." She waved at Mandy to follow her into her office.

The principal sat at her desk, and Mandy on a large couch facing her. "I'm glad you came actually, Ms. Knox."

"What do you mean?"

"I've been wanting to talk to you again about Callie." Ms. Blacksmith shuffled some papers into a folder, cleaning her desk as they spoke. "Sorry, I could never keep a clean workstation, even as a professional."

Mandy ignored her comment. "Do you know where Callie is?"

"No," the principal said curtly. "In fact, we haven't seen her much this semester. She has been writing herself out of school a lot this year. Now that she's eighteen, she has taken full advantage of being able to sign herself out from school for being *sick*."

"Mr. Greyson said she ditched his science class today. Did she even come to school today?"

"I'd have to sort through our records to find out, Ms. Knox. It's not uncommon for students being less present at school during the last week. Mr. Greyson said she also skipped her final test, though he assured me that he would pass her in good faith."

Mandy could feel her heart beating out of her chest. "Is my daughter not graduating?"

"I was planning on calling you this week," Ms. Blacksmith said. "I think I can get her other teachers to agree to pass her as well, so long as she writes a make-up exam during the summer and passes. Otherwise, no, she won't."

Mandy laughed. "I don't get this, none of it. This isn't Callie!"

Ms. Blacksmith smiled thinly. "That's what I heard from her teachers as well. I didn't know your daughter very well, and unfortunately, it seems I met her during a rough time. Are things okay at home?"

Mandy could feel her blood rising. "What are you saying? My daughter goes from being an amazing student to—and you ask me what's happening at home? And, what? You were going to call me? When? None of you called me! Why?"

"Ms. Knox, please lower your voice. Please!"

The stern voice of the principal was enough to calm Mandy's nerves for a moment. "I should have been notified," she continued in a reasonable tone. "If she wasn't showing up, dropping drama, not attending her finals. I should have known."

"We did!" Ms. Blacksmith said sternly. "We spoke a month ago." She turned from Mandy, flicking through several file folders behind her.

"What are you talking about?" Mandy asked, nearly in rage.

Ms. Blacksmith turned back to her, opening a yellow folder. She sifted through some paperwork until she found what she was looking for. "We spoke on May third. I told you about her concerning behavior. And look here." She pointed at another form with handwritten notes. "We talked a month before that in April as well." Mandy unfolded her hands, letting them slip beside her. "Along with this, we send report cards as well. We *have* reached out to you, so please don't say that we haven't tried here at Cranston High."

Mandy stood up, not knowing what to do. "Where is my daughter?"

Ms. Blacksmith stood and waved towards the door. "I'm sorry. I must get ready for my next appointment."

"Where is she?"

Ms. Blacksmith let out a sigh. "We are not babysitters here, Ms. Knox. This is a high school. Perhaps you should call Mr. Knox."

Mandy stormed out the principal's office before making a scene. She continued down the main hall where all the photos of graduating students mocked her on the way out of the building.

CHAPTER FIVE

Mandy hung up the phone with more force than needed as soon as she heard the woman say, "We don't have a Callie Knox here."

In the Essex County, there were only two hospitals that Callie could have wound up in, and both confirmed she wasn't there. She opened the phone book and looked up other hospitals that were in the state.

She wouldn't be there though, right? Why would she be beyond Essex? This doesn't make sense.

None of it did. Callie, a grade A student, was now nearly flunking out of high school. Not only that, but now she was ditching school entirely. Drama was the one thing she loved most about school, and she'd quit that as well.

Mandy picked up the phone again, staring at the phone book, and put in the number for High River Hospital. It was at least an eight-hour drive away from Cranston, but Mandy knew the hospital well, as it had an inpatient detox center. Mandy had driven herself there, while Callie was left with her father for those two months.

Memories flooded Mandy as she waited for someone to pick up the phone. Those first few nights of detox were the worst. Her body had almost felt like it was going to curl up and die as she begged the staff to let her drink.

Finally, the symptoms resolved, and so did the urge to drink after a few weeks. She was proud of herself when she completed the two-month program.

"You can do this, Mom. You're strong!" Mandy remembered the words of encouragement Callie had given her before she left. Callie had never had told her to do it for her.

Why?

Mandy knew it was because Callie thought she wasn't going to be able to do it at all. Callie had likely suspected her mother wasn't going to stop drinking. She knew she wasn't strong. It was a miracle that it happened.

"Hello. High River Hospital. How can I help you?"

Mandy hung up the phone immediately. She took a deep breath before picking it back up and dialing his number.

After a few rings he picked up. "Yeah?"

It always bothered her when her ex-husband would pick up the phone this way. It was as if he was already annoyed at the inconvenience of having to pick up the phone.

"Hey, Steve, it's me," Mandy said in a low voice.

"Mandy?" If his voice didn't sound irritated when he first picked up, it certainly did now. "What do you want?"

"Nothing."

Steve laughed. "You want nothing? I'm about to head out to deliver a load, so I don't have time for games. What do you want?"

Mandy breathed out before continuing, "Callie said she was going to be with you this weekend. Is she with you now?"

"Callie said what? She's not here." Steve sighed. "Shit. Did I miss her graduation?"

"No," Mandy said. "So she's not with you? She said you were going to take her out to dinner."

"I have no clue what you're talking about," he said. "So, where is she?"

Mandy could feel a tear forming. "I don't... The school said she wasn't there today."

"She ditched? So you don't know where my daughter is?" Steve asked, raising his voice. Mandy could feel her heart beat faster. She had heard this tone in his voice before. She'd found out the hard way what would happen immediately after he raised his voice. Thankfully, he was nowhere near her.

"I don't—I'm not sure—"

"Mandy! Is she with a friend?" he asked.

"I don't think so."

She heard the sound of a bang on the other end of the phone. "What does that mean, Mandy?" Steve almost yelled. "Do you not keep track of where she is?"

Mandy felt lightheaded. She almost felt as if she was going to pass out on the floor. She looked around the living room. The picture of Callie and her at Disneyland caught her attention.

"I did a hell of a lot of better than you with keeping track of her," Mandy yelled into the phone.

For a moment, there was silence between them.

"Calm down!" Steve yelled. "She's probably out with her friends or something. It's the end of the school year. You remember how we were around her age? Call her friends."

"I don't have their numbers."

"Get them!" Steve yelled. "Fuck, Mandy. I have to leave. This is my regular load. I can't afford to not make it on time. Handle this shit! Wait, did you guys fight or anything?"

"No, nothing like that."

"I knew she should have stayed with me," Steve said. "Teenager daughters and their mothers never get along."

"She wanted to stay with me!" Mandy said defiantly.

Silence again.

"Did you call the police or anything?" Steve asked in a calmer tone.

"No. Not yet."

Steve didn't respond and was silent again. Mandy thought for a moment he had hung up.

"You have my beeper number." Steve said. "Figure this out. Page me. I'm coming over when I'm back in on Sunday, and when I do, I expect to see my daughter. I'll take her back to my place, away from whatever bullshit you have going on with her. And I expect you to cut out that sassy tongue of yours too."

The phone connection dropped, followed by the sounds of

beeps from the phone. Mandy sat on the couch for a moment, wondering what to do next and trying to calm her heartbeat. Steve had a way of getting to her, scaring her even. She felt like she was still married to him in that moment, worried what he would be like when he came home from work after being away a few nights on the road.

She knew she had to call the police, as much as dreaded it.

She went into the kitchen, poured some water into a kettle, and put it on the stove to heat it up. As terrible as instant coffee was, she needed it to comfort her in that moment. She found the coffee tin on top of the kitchen garbage and plucked it out.

I just need to collect myself before I call the police.

Mandy opened the front door of the house and took a few steps out onto their wooden porch. It was beautiful outside. There was slight breeze, cooling off the June afternoon. A fly flew past her ear, and Mandy waved the bug off. She looked to both sides of the street, almost expecting to seeing Callie casually strolling down the block back home. Instead, a few cars whizzed by.

She heard the fly again and felt it land on her bare leg. She brushed it off and looked down, noticing a second fly was on her other leg.

The kettle on the stove whistled for attention. Callie turned to the open front door and was slightly annoyed that she'd forgotten to shut the door. She hated flies in the house.

Mandy took a few steps, waving off several flies as she did, and stopped suddenly right outside her front door. She stood on her light grey welcome mat, noticing a large black stain. The kitchen kettle whistled louder but no longer had her attention. She looked closer at the stain, noticing it wasn't just the welcome mat ruined, but a large area of her front porch was dirtied with the same color. Kneeling now, she noticed it wasn't black in color, but a dark shade of red.

Mandy covered her mouth while the flies aggressively buzzed around her.

CHAPTER SIX

Mandy sat on her couch in the living room. She peered outside at her porch as officers taped off the premises with police tape.

Blood.

Mandy tried to think of anything else but what she just saw. She'd called 911 in a panic, barely making any sense to the operator. Taking some time to get the words out, Mandy finally yelled, "Someone killed her!"

Within ten minutes, the first officer showed up, asking her to stay inside in her living room. She sat on her couch, watching him as he reviewed the bloodstained welcome mat in front of the house and surrounding porch. The officer spoke into the radio on his shoulder, saying something into it that she couldn't hear.

It's her blood.

Soon after, more officers arrived. Mandy could see some of her neighbors gathering outside, curiously buzzing around her home.

Callie's blood.

The front door opened, then a tall man and slightly shorter woman came inside. The tall, dark-skinned man took out a gold badge from around his neck, showing the officer inside the kitchen. The officer waved them in and nodded towards Mandy's direction, whispering something.

The woman maintained eye contact with Mandy as she stepped in. She didn't come off like a detective. The woman was tall, around five-eleven, with a loose fitting trench coat, dark dress pants, and a white shirt underneath. She had dark hair in a short, almost buzzed cut, but it didn't look bad on her. She looked to be a little over thirty, if Mandy guessed.

The tall man had a different aura to him. He appeared slightly older than the woman. He was well over a foot taller than her and wore a black blazer, white shirt, and dark jeans. His face was stern, with a strong jawline. It was as if a well-dressed football player had entered her home.

The woman was the first to speak. "Hi, Ms. Knox. I'm Detective Alda Lane, and this is my partner, Tony Ferguson." Detective Ferguson nodded his head slightly. "We're part of the major crimes unit."

Mandy couldn't stop the tears from escaping. Detective Ferguson took out a Kleenex from his blazer pocket and handed it to her. Mandy wiped her eyes, fought back the army of them that were coming, and thanked him.

"Right now," Ferguson said, "we're considering your daughter to be missing."

"But—" Mandy said, pointing towards the door.

"We will treat this case with the utmost care," Detective Lane said quickly. "Because we don't know what happened yet, the police label it that way. Rest assured though, we will figure out what happened."

It suddenly dawned on Mandy that they couldn't consider it a homicide because there was no body. She pictured Callie's lifeless body on the front porch, illuminated by only the moonlight. She pictured her killer, shrouded by the darkness of the night, dragging her daughter's corpse off her front steps.

Lane broke her thoughts. "When was the last time you saw Callie?"

"Two nights ago," she admitted, embarrassed. "She said she was going to meet a friend for a study session but didn't come home."

Lane held her pen tighter. "Which friend was this again?"

Mandy sighed. "It doesn't mat—I mean, she didn't go to a friend's house to study, at least. I went to the school and they told me she's been skipping classes. Apparently, the finals are all done, so there were no tests to study for."

Lane put her lips together. She reached behind her for one of the kitchen tables chairs and brought it closer to the living room, sitting across from Mandy. Detective Ferguson continued to stand, observing Mandy and noticing the pictures around the living room.

"Well, what's was the name of the friend whose house you thought she was going to?" Lane continued.

"Jessica," Mandy answered. She lowered her head, trying to remember. "I'm, not sure what her last name is."

"Who are some of her other friends?" Lane asked. She got ready to jot down some names, waiting patiently for Mandy to answer.

"I'm not sure," Mandy said. Ferguson looked down at her briefly, then back at the picture of Callie and Mandy from Disneyland.

"What about places she likes to go to?" Lane asked.

"I already checked the school," Mandy said. "I thought maybe her drama teacher would know something." She pointed at a picture of Mandy on stage. "That's her in a school play."

"What's the drama teacher's name?" Ferguson asked.

"Rand Peterson. I think Rand is short for Randall."

"Have you guys been fighting, Ms. Knox?" Ferguson asked, fixing the crooked picture frame of Callie and her.

"No! I didn't do anything to her," Mandy said.

"That's not what he meant, Ms. Knox," Lane said softly. "We just want to know if there was any friction between you two. Was there a reason why she would have wanted to lie to you about where she was going?"

"No, I don't think so."

"Did she have a boyfriend, or a boy she was seeing?" Ferguson asked.

Mandy shook her head. "No. She would have told me something like that."

"But you did say she stopped going to school and lied to you about it," Ferguson noted. "Are you sure she would have told you?"

Mandy lowered her head. "I...don't know."

Lane put her hand out to Mandy's arm, grabbing it softly. When she did, she noticed a colorful butterfly tattoo on her forearm. "I have to ask, and again, we don't know what happened to Callie, but do you know anyone who would have wanted to hurt her? Anyone at all?"

Mandy shook her head again. "No. I don't think so." Lane stood up from the chair and put her logbook into her jacket pocket. "Wait, there has been someone calling the house. On the night she left, Callie picked up the phone and hung it up, saying they had the wrong number. The next day, someone called again and just breathed into the phone. I knew someone was there, but they didn't say anything. It happened one more time as well, only that time, I heard a woman laughing. She didn't say anything and just hung up."

Detective Ferguson nodded and asked Mandy for the approximate times they called the home. "We'll look into that, thank you."

"What about her father?" Lane asked. "Where is he?"

"Steve and I are divorced. He sees Callie now and then. He's a truck driver. I called him before I called the police, but he didn't know where she was either."

"Why isn't he here today, Ms. Knox?" Lane asked.

"He's driving. He told me he's on the road for a few days. I can give you his beeper number."

"We have his contact info," Detective Lane said. "Do you know if Callie and her father have any issues with each other?"

"We don't really talk about him." Mandy lowed her head. "I didn't tell him about..." She pointed towards the front porch. "What am I going to do?"

Ferguson looked at Mandy, clenching his jaw. "So, just to be sure, you don't have any idea where your daughter was the night she left? Who she might have seen? Friends or a boyfriend?"

I don't know anything about my daughter anymore.

Mandy shook her head. "No." She let the detective's words

sink into her soul. All the questions were jabs to her heart. She could see it on their faces, especially Detective Ferguson's. *'Why don't you know?'* She could hear her ex-husband's voice threatening her with finding Callie.

"What was she wearing the night she left?" Lane asked.

Mandy gave a thin smile. Finally, a question she knew the answer to.

How pathetic.

"She was wearing a yellow dress, and she had this yellow scrunchie for her hair." Mandy smiled again, but this time, it was at thinking of how beautiful her daughter was.

"Do you have any pictures with her in the dress?" Detective Ferguson asked. "Or any recent pictures we could use?"

"I'm not sure about the dress, but I'll look."

"Ms. Knox," Lane said, getting her attention. "Some of our officers would like to look through your home, especially Callie's bedroom. Any concerns with that?"

Mandy shook her head no but remembered her gun. "Actually, can you have them look through Callie's room only?"

"Any concerns with us looking through the rest of your home, Ms. Knox?" Ferguson asked.

"I'd prefer just her room, please."

Ferguson looked at Lane briefly and back at Mandy. "I'm sorry, Ms. Knox, but with a possible crime scene outside your front door, we do have probable cause to search your home."

"Sorry, of course," Mandy said quickly. "Do what you have to." Mandy looked at her front door, worried about what was staining her front porch. She looked at Detective Lane. "That amount of blood. If someone loses that much blood—I mean, that has to mean they—"

"We don't know anything right now, Ms. Knox," Lane said again. "Is there someone you can call? Any family or friend you could see tonight? We're going to be a few hours at your home, and it's good to have someone with you right now."

"Thanks," Mandy answered curtly.

All I have is Callie.

The front door opened, and several cops in uniform entered the home. Detective Ferguson pointed them towards certain areas of the home.

"What about a diary?" Detective Lane asked her. "Does your daughter keep a diary somewhere in her room or the home?"

What did she really know about Callie after the last few days? Mandy was scared to answer anything now, for fear that it would sink in deeper how little she knew about her only child. She pictured Callie as a little girl, prancing in her small white dresses, putting on a dance show for her. She remembered putting her to sleep when she was a toddler, and how scared she was of monsters outside the house. She was always a bit anxious as a child. When she was a young teenager, Mandy would peek in her daughter's room, and she would always be looking at random books that were not required for class homework. She remembered the first guy Callie had a crush on in the seventh grade, and how she talked about how tall he was for his age and his handsome face. Never did she see or hear of a diary. Callie herself seemed like an open book.

"No," Mandy answered.

Three months before missing.

How do you know if a boy likes you? Actually likes you.
Fin stared at my chest for what felt like over a minute. That's lust, I know that much at least.
Still, I didn't exactly hate it. He was one of the hottest guys at Cranston High. He graduated last year, but a lot of girls still talk about him, especially Jessica.
Jessica wouldn't like if I told her that her boy toy wanted to play with me.
Sure, Fin is hot and I think about him too sometimes, but out of all the boys out there, I wouldn't allow myself to let him be my first.
Maybe he could be my first mistake. The one who I go to after a heartbreak from my actual first love to make it all better for a few moments.
My first regret.
None of this matters right now. In a few months, Cranston will be a distant memory. My next step is university or college, after that, who knows? Maybe Hollywood or New York.
Wherever the limelight brings me is where I'll be living.
I suppose I won't even have time to have a first love or a first anything.
If I did, I could have one of those relationships that the tabloids love to write about someday. Someday.
Uncle James is teaching me to drive now. I should have gotten my learner's permit a year ago. Eighteen and no license!
For a moment, I thought I caught Uncle James staring at me too.
"You look just like your mother when she was your age, Callie."
How many times have I heard him say that? Rhetorical question.
I wonder sometimes how my mother will take it when I leave…
Whatever her reaction is, Dad's will be the complete opposite. I can't wait to get away from that man. Yesterday he—

Journal pages ripped.

One month before missing

Nobody knows the real me.

Out of everyone in my life, maybe Steph has the closest idea, but even with her, I change who I am.

I'm not even sure if I know who I am anymore.

I wish I could go back in a time machine to when I was nine, before my budding breasts were even a problem for me.

Now, everything is sex.

Sex.

Who have you done? Banged? How many notches are on your bedpost?

Who cares?

Fuck my dad.

Fuck Fin.

Fuck Jessica.

Especially fuck my piece of shit uncle.

Fuck Mom for holding me back. I'm tired of being her keeper.

I'm tired of everything.

I looked back at some of my entries before writing today, laughing at how stupid I was.

College? University?

No thanks.

That talent agent was right about only one thing—I needed more life experience.

I'll show them all what I can be.

CHAPTER SEVEN

Detective Alda Lane

Detective Alda Lane left Ms. Knox's home, exiting through the side door. On her way to her black Mustang, she took a moment to look at the crime scene experts looking at the dried blood on the front porch. She sat inside her car, writing a few more notes. Detective Ferguson sauntered to the passenger side, awkwardly lowering his body to get inside.

"Alda, I'm a fan of sports cars too, but for the love of god, sign out a car that a man can sit in." Ferguson managed to sit inside, his head tilted to avoid hitting the top, looking even more uncomfortable.

"Stop bitching, Ferg," she said with a smile.

"At some point, I'm driving. If I'm going to be stuck inside this tuna can, I want the wheel." Ferg shut the car door, looking at Alda for pity.

Alda sighed. "I know you're new to the major crimes unit, but you'll find out real soon that there's no way that's happening."

Ferg shook his head in disapproval. "I heard a lot about you when I started." He waited a moment to see if Alda would say something. Alda Lane didn't answer. She was used to having new partners. Ferguson wouldn't be her last. "What do you think about Ms. Knox?"

"You're the rookie," Alda said. "Let me hear what you think."

"If it weren't for the blood, I'd think her daughter was a runaway."

Alda nodded her head in approval. It wasn't unheard of for young women to leave Cranston the instant they could. Parents got in the way of that. Usually, there was a note though. This time, there was only blood.

"There was a noticeable number of empty hangers in her closet too," Alda said. "Ms. Knox said she left with a backpack."

"To *study*," Ferg said. "Talk about a woman who knows nothing about her own kid."

Alda hated that comment. Nobody knew anybody, not really. Nobody knew what someone else was truly capable of. Nobody knew the darkness that lurked right below the surface of their friends or family. Suddenly, there was a cold body on the floor, and the killer was someone nobody thought could have done it. Ferg should have known this already.

"She's eighteen," Alda said with a hard tone. "How much did your parents really know about what you were doing at that age?'

"They knew my friends," he said raising a finger. "My girl-friends, usually." He raised another finger. "They knew the sports I was into, and what I liked and disliked. That woman knew nothing."

Alda nodded her head. "She was right about one thing—no diary."

"No diary, yes," Ferg said with a forgiving tone. "I noticed you didn't bring up her daughter's criminal background to Amanda Knox, her recent open liquor fines."

"I doubt Ms. Knox would know anything about that also." Alda sighed.

"It almost looks like a major artery was opened with the amount of blood on the front porch. Callie Knox would have been killed while walking into her home, and her body moved."

"Uniforms are canvassing the block. Hopefully, someone saw something."

"So where do we start on this, Lane?" Ferg asked.

"I want to get Steve Knox in a room. Interview him. See

what he has to say."

Ferg smiled. "You're going to have to tell me what's up with you and this guy. You almost volunteered us to work this case after they said the last name of this girl, *Knox.* You mentioned Steve Knox several times on the way over here. So what is it?"

"I know your new to this county, but I'm sure even in Philadelphia, you heard about the killings of those girls we found in the woods out here?"

Alda turned the ignition, the engine roaring to life. She revved the engine once to satisfy herself. She looked at Ferg, cramped up in the passenger seat, and smiles. "Well, we got some time to kill before getting back to station. I'll fill you in on everything you need to know about Steve Knox."

CHAPTER EIGHT

Mandy

Mandy lay on her couch. She had plopped herself there when the police showed up and told her to sit, and she hadn't moved since, even though it had been hours since they'd left. A few days ago, she'd lain on the very same couch, wondering how her life could get any worse.

How stupid she felt.

That day was the last she saw Callie, and she knew it would be the last time she ever would again. Callie had attempted to cheer her up that day. Callie always had that job. Whenever her life was going bad, Callie was always there to support her. No matter what, it was always her and Callie.

Now what were they?

Nothing. The dried river of blood outside her front door stood as a reminder of that. Mandy couldn't bear to get off the couch, because she knew she would immediately run to the front door to see what was left of her daughter.

She pictured her body, cold, blue, and sprawled out in the middle of nowhere, waiting to be found.

Maybe she just ran away. How good could these cops be? They didn't even find my gun in the closet!

Her instincts told her otherwise though. She knew something terrible had happened to Callie. She didn't need a puddle of her daughter's blood to prove it.

Where will they find her body?

Who had done this?

She barely knew her daughter now. How could she find out more?

Mandy stood off the couch, staring at the pictures on the living room wall again. The pictures taunted her with Callie's presence.

The picture of the two of them at Disneyland was the worst. Then she saw the one of her in the play as the Virgin Mary and hated herself even more.

If only I knew her friends, I would have been able to do something. I could have given the police something. Some information to help them find her.

Maybe that would be worse.

Perhaps it was better for Mandy to never find out what had happened to her daughter. That way, she could stay hopeful that she was somewhere, thinking of her.

The police had said items were missing from her room. She could have run away.

Mandy opened the front door and looked down. The dark dried blood on the wooden deck and welcome mat brought an end to her daydreams.

Mandy slammed her front door and ran into her kitchen. She called his number out of desperation. After several rings, it went to his answering machine.

"You got Steve's machine," her ex-husband's deep voice said. "I'm not here."

After the beep, Mandy breathed into the phone. "Steve, if you're home, pick up." Even when they were together, Steve would never pick up the phone. He rarely let Mandy or Callie answer it, telling them to let the machine screen the calls while he drank his beer. "Steve! Answer the phone. Please!" She hung up and called his beeper, leaving a message for him to return her call.

She sat at the kitchen counter, lowering her head on the hard surface. She wanted to bash her head against the laminate counter. Tears began to form in her eyes.

She pictured herself, her *old self*, going straight to the bar. After her divorce with Steve, that was one of the little comforts she'd had. Steve had had a fight with the manager at this dive bar in town, and the cops had been called. After that, he never went there again. In a small town like Cranston, it was nice to know which places she could claim all to herself. She pictured herself going to the bartender, then asking for a shot of whiskey and a bottle of beer to chase it with. She could almost taste the sweet burn of the liquor on her tongue.

The phone rang, and Mandy immediately picked up. "Hello?" Nobody answered. "Hello?!" The silence on the other end of the phone brought her to rage. "Who the fuck is this? Tell me now!"

"Mandy?" It wasn't Steve's deep voice, or the woman from yesterday. His voice was comforting, sweet even. It was better than any whiskey in town. "What's wrong? Are you okay?"

"James! No-no I'm not. It's Callie."

James laughed. "What, did she get a B again?"

Mandy let out a sigh of desperation. "She's missing. I think she's dead." The phone was silent for a few moments. "She's dead," she whispered. "Can you come over? I need you."

"I'm on my way."

When James arrived, he entered through the side door, as he usually would whenever he visited. Most the time, it would be when Callie was out of the home. Mandy couldn't risk James knocking on the front door all the time and had given him a key. He would typically dress in darker clothes with a baseball cap, in case any nosey neighbors saw anything.

Mandy spent the first twenty minutes or so weeping in his arms on the couch. He attempted to get his lover to say what had happened, but it was no use. Mandy made no sense. Between her sobs, she could barely form any sentences.

When she finally calmed, she told him everything. How she came home that night after seeing him and noticed Callie's light was still on, but didn't knock on her door. How the next day, Callie didn't come home from school. How she went to the school to find her and found out all the things she didn't know was happening in her daughter's life.

"So why do you think she's dead?" James asked calmly. "It sounds like she's been going through something. She could have run away, as silly as that sounds."

"I wish," Mandy said, controlling her tears. She grabbed his hand, guiding him to the front door, and opened it slowly. She looked away and pointed at the mess on the deck.

James covered his mouth. "No, that can't be."

"It is." Mandy said, wiping away a tear. "The police left a few hours ago."

James was silent a moment. "Do they know who did it?"

"No. I mean, I don't think so." It had been running through her head all day.

James brushed a lock of Mandy's hair to the side of her face. His hand was warm, comforting. He kissed the side of her head. "You thought I was someone else on the phone," he said. "Why?" Mandy told him about the random phone calls and the woman who laughed the one time.

As if the universe listened to Mandy, the phone rang loudly, making her almost jump. "I can't...I can't answer it."

James stood up. "It's okay. It could be the police." He picked up the phone, but immediately stood silent. He put his hand over the receiver and looked at Mandy. It was as if he had seen a ghost.

"Steve," he whispered, reaching out to Mandy with the phone. She picked it up quickly.

"Hey," she said loudly.

"What are you doing?" Steve asked with an annoyed tone. "I got you calling me, then the police. Where's Callie? What the fuck is going on, Amanda?"

Mandy couldn't bring herself to say the words. She stood there, her mouth open, but no words escaped. "I don't know," she finally managed.

"No shit," Steve blasted back. "Why are the cops calling me?"

"She's dead! She's dead, Steve! The cops want to tell you about your dead daughter! Call them back right away." Mandy hung up the phone, nearly breaking it.

James stood beside her, wrapping his arms around her. "My brother is something else," he said.

"Don't remind me you two are related," she said, shrugging off his arms. "Don't remind me how much of a shitty person I am right now! That I'm the type of woman to fuck her ex-husband's brother."

He looked surprised. "Tell me what you want me to do here, Mandy. Do you want me to stay? Leave? Whatever you need."

"I'm sorry, I'm just… I don't know. I don't know what I am right now. I just wish I wasn't *here* anymore."

"What do you mean?" James asked, grabbing her waist and pulling her closer. He kissed her softly on the lips. James' touch would typically bring Mandy into overdrive, but tonight, it did nothing. "It's okay," he said. "I can go. I'll come back tomorrow, and —"

"No! Sorry, please don't," Mandy said desperately, grabbing his hand and burying herself into his chest. "I need you tonight. Stay with me."

He patted her head and kissed her hair. "Okay."

One month before missing.

"You've got the look."
The talent agent had something else right, I suppose.
Sexy, playful, young. All attributes that an actress needs before they open their mouth in an audition.
It's time I used it to my advantage.
In Cranston, looks only get boys' attention, like Fin. I tell him about my plans for Hollywood. He wants in. He could make it there too, maybe we both could. Steph would come just for the ride!
We could pack our bags in his car and just drive until we see the large sign over Hollywood Hills.
How many celebrities have you heard of who started off working as a waitress until they were discovered?
Bruce Willis was a bartender before he made it.
What would be my story?
Then you have my mom. She's been a waitress her whole life, and where did that get her?
I'd rather not answer that.
If I tell her, she will find some way of stopping me, directly or indirectly.
Maybe she'd even start drinking again.
That's her problem, not mine anymore. That's anyone else's problem, besides mine.
High school is almost over, and then I'm free. I'm not sure why I'm waiting for school to end at this point. I barely go after what happened.
School really just gets in the way.
I need more life experience.
Love you, Mom, but I can't get that with you, here in Cranston.

CHAPTER NINE

Detective Alda Lane

Alda knocked loudly on Ms. Knox's front door. She pressed the doorbell but didn't hear any kind of a ring, so she knocked again, louder.

"What kind of a police knock is that, Lane?" Ferguson asked with a smile. He pounded hard on the door. His loud thumps didn't stop until they heard the lock of the front door open. Mandy Knox opened her front door, wiping the sleep from her eyes, wearing a raggedy robe. It only took a moment for Alda to notice the bare, hairy foot of a man lying on her couch.

Ms. Knox looked down at Alda's feet on her welcome mat. "Oh no," Mandy said, covering her mouth. "What? You found her?" Ms. Knox began to cry, her body almost shaking. The hairy foot started to move in the background.

"No, Ms. Knox," Alda reassured her. "We have some good news."

Mandy closed her front door and stood on her front porch, unable to keep her eyes from weeping.

Detective Ferguson took out some Kleenex from his suit jacket, giving it to Ms. Knox. "Pig's blood," he blurted out, perhaps in an attempt to make her stop crying.

Amanda Knox suddenly looked frozen. The door opened, and a slim man looked at Amanda, then at her and Ferg. "What happened? Did you find her?"

Callie pointed at the dried blood on the deck. "So this...

It's..."

"That's right, Ms. Knox," Detective Ferguson said. "It's pig's blood."

"Our lab confirmed it this morning, Ms. Knox," Alda said with a thin smile.

"So what does this mean?" the handsome man asked.

"Can we go inside and talk?" Alda asked.

"Of course," Ms. Knox said. She opened the door for them to enter. Alda noticed the bed sheets on the couch and the bedheads of Ms. Knox and her *friend.*

The man went into the kitchen. "Can I offer you guys some coffee?"

"No thank you, sir," Detective Ferguson replied. "I'm sorry, but are you Steve Knox?"

"No," Alda answered. "We're still trying to get ahold of your ex-husband, Ms. Knox. So if you do hear from him, please let him know." Amanda nodded her head.

"I'm Callie's uncle, James." He reached out his hand to Detective Ferguson, who shook it.

Ferguson looked at Amanda Knox. "Your brother?"

Amanda and the man named James exchanged a quick glance. "No," he answered. "Steve is my brother."

"I know, it's confusing," Amanda said. "I never changed my last name after the divorce. I don't have a reason why, it was just something I never got around to, I guess."

Alda bit her lip with that news. She could feel Ferguson's stare in the back of her head, having the same thoughts she did. "I came to console her as best I could, after she told me what happened," James continued. "But" —he looked at Amanda— "this is great news."

Amanda didn't respond and looked at Alda. "So what does this mean now? What happens with her case?"

"It's considered a missing persons case now," Ferguson said promptly.

"Don't worry, Ms. Knox," Alda said softly. "Detective Ferguson and I will still be working on finding your daughter."

"But you…you're the murder police? So why would you still be involved if you think nothing is wrong with Callie?"

"We handle major crimes," Alda said, agreeing, "but there's no reason to suspect foul play or anything like that now. The pig's blood is…odd, but it doesn't mean your daughter is in danger or harmed."

"Do you know any reason why someone would dump pig's blood on your front door?" Detective Ferguson asked. "Maybe that wasn't intended for Callie, but you, Ms. Knox. Is there anyone who has anything against you that could explain the pig's blood?"

Amanda Knox shook her head from side to side. "No…I mean, I don't think so."

"Mr. Knox, can you think of anything?" Detective Ferguson asked James.

The uncle shook his head as well.

"Well, if you can think of anything, please let us know," Alda said to them. "We do have more to share though." Alda reached into her long jacket pockets and grabbed the picture of the young teenager. "This is Steph Moore, and apparently, she and your daughter are known to be best friends." Amanda Knox grabbed the photo and stared at the girl.

"That can't be," Amanda said, surprised. Alda looked down at the photo. She had long brunette hair that was frizzled in the picture. Her midriff was showing below her low cut tank top, with a short skirt to match. She had what appeared to be a nose ring. The minimal clothes she wore were all dark. Steph Moore looked stoned out of her mind in the picture. The black lipstick topped off the unique look.

"Teachers tell us they are close," Fergsuon said.

"Which ones?" Amanda asked.

"Mr. Greyson." Amanda looked dumbfounded. "Steph Moore is also missing. We are presuming that her and your daughter are together. Steph's mother confirmed the last time she saw her daughter was with Callie."

"Do you know if your daughter had any presence online?" Alda asked.

"Online?" asked Amanda, confused.

"Yes," Alda said. "The world wide web. Maybe a blog or something like that?"

Amanda Knox still appeared confused. "We don't even have internet in our home. It was too expensive for me."

Alda handed James Knox her card. "If you can think of anybody with anything against Amanda or Callie, please let me know, even if it's something small. Sometimes, it's the small details that break a case."

"Definitely, I will." James grabbed the card, reading it. "Thank you, Detective Lane."

She faced Amanda. "We are still tracking down more leads, but we strongly believe your daughter and Ms. Moore are together. I will let you know when I have more, but call me if you have any questions or news to share."

"You can clean your front porch now, Ms. Knox," Detective Ferguson said. "It's no longer considered a crime scene."

Amanda Knox and James Knox thanked the detectives before they left her house. As they walked towards the unmarked police cruiser, Alda could feel the laser eyes of Ferg on her still.

"Don't even start," she said.

"Well," Ferg said with a laugh, "I'll put in my notes that the friendly uncle had a sleepover." Alda didn't respond. They got into the car, Alda taking the driver's seat, again. Ferg didn't even attempt to fight her for the spot this time, sitting in the passenger side immediately. "I'm just saying," he continued, "I have better shit to do than this runaway shit. I mean, she's right, we are the *murder police.*"

"I want to see this one out, rookie. Got a problem with that?"

She could see Ferguson bite his lip with that remark. "I told you to cut that. I'm no rookie. I've been a homicide cop for two years out in Philly before coming here. I don't care to get involved in the Jerry Springer shit going on this county."

Alda typically enjoyed getting a rise out of her coworkers. She enjoyed the number of partners she'd had throughout her time in major crimes. Those babies with a badge acted tough, but the moment you gave it back to them as good as they gave it out, they cried to the chief.

Ferg was different. Even though they'd only worked together for a little over a month, she actually liked him, even respected him. Not ever had he made any sexist comments to her like the others. He kept it professional, which was a hard thing to do with someone Alda Lane.

"Sorry," Alda said. "Like I said though, I need to see this one out."

"Because of Steve Knox?"

"That's right. I told you why." Alda noticed how disappointed Ferguson looked. "Look, if you keep me as your partner, I owe you one for this, okay?"

"That's fine, Lane. But when we find this girl at her boyfriend's house or LA or wherever she ran to, I'm going to still enjoy saying I told you so."

CHAPTER TEN

Mandy

Mandy Knox let in sink in that her daughter was not dead.

Pig's blood. Why pig's blood?

"What's wrong? James asked her. He held her tight around her waist. "She's okay. Callie is okay!"

"Yeah," Mandy said, "but where is she?"

James put his head down. "Listen, this may be hard, but she must have run away. Cranston is too small for a girl like Callie."

"Not like this though," Mandy said, shaking her head. "She would have left a note, told me, gave me a hint, something."

"If she told you, would you have let her leave?"

Mandy stood quietly. She knew the answer was no, but she didn't like the reason why. Without Callie, who was she? Her life was always a train wreck, and the only thing that kept her from complete derailment was Callie. She needed her. How could she just leave?

"And that girl, Steph Moore?" Mandy said with a sigh. "Who is that? That's not the type of girl Callie would be friends with. She looked like a character out of a vampire book, with her dark clothes and lipstick. I just—"

James held her hand. "It's going to be okay. We know that she's safe at least."

"How do we know that?"

James let go of her hand. "She packed a bag full of clothes, and now she's not here. She said she was going to study but didn't." James pointed at the picture on the wall of Callie as Mary in the school play. "We know what she wants to do. She has always wanted to be an actress. She's probably in Hollywood or some city like that. Stop being blind, Mandy. Your daughter ran away."

Mandy shook her head. "No. She didn't. She wouldn't do that. I may not know everything about my daughter, but I know that much. Something is very wrong!"

"Calm down," James said, putting up his arms. For a moment, she caught a glimpse of his brother Steve, raising his arms before one of them would land on her face.

"Don't you dare tell me to calm down!" Mandy barked back. She wasn't scared of him anymore.

"Okay, sorry," James said, lowering his hands to his side. "I want to help, though."

"The cops, they asked if my daughter has some kind of blog online. I don't even know how you do that, but maybe that's a start. Maybe this Steph Moore does. Hell, maybe Callie does too." Mandy lowered her head. "I know I heard that last name before too —Moore. Have you heard of it? Do you know any Moore in town?"

"No," James said, "but there's a net café nearby. We can check there."

"Net café?" Mandy asked, confused.

James laughed. "It's a place where you pay to get internet access. Sometimes they have drinks."

"How do you even know about these places?" Mandy asked with a thin smile.

They left her house. James opened the passenger door of his white Escalade for Mandy to get in, then sauntered to the driver's side. He put on his dark sunglasses before turning the ignition.

"It's only a fifteen-minute drive," he reminded Mandy.

They parked outside of a strip mall that was on the main street of downtown Cranston, in front of Cyber Café. The storefront was mostly red with streaks of yellow. James opened the front door, and Mandy went inside. Inside, the store was cluttered with rows of computers, half of them being occupied.

"Hi," the young woman at the front counter said to her. "Can I help you?"

Mandy walked up to the counter shyly. "I'm not really sure how this works."

The young woman shoved her long curly blonde hair to one side, revealing a name tag that said 'Bethany.' "It only seems like a lot, but I can help you."

James walked up beside Mandy, taking off his sunglasses. When he noticed the busty young woman named Bethany, his smirk vanished from his face.

"James?" she asked. "What are you—"

"Hey, Beth," he said in a somber tone. "Can we get a computer in the corner?"

"That's all you're going to say to me?" Bethany asked with dismay. "You just stopped talking to me, just like that. You didn't return my calls."

James looked around, taking a moment to see Mandy's glare at him. "Can we not do this please? It's been six months."

Bethany pointed at a computer in the back of the store. "You can use that one." The young woman looked at Mandy. "I'm not sure how you know this man, but he's scum. Pure scum." She looked back at James with a scowl. "At least you're finding woman your own age now, scumbag!"

James didn't respond and pushed on Mandy's back, gently guiding her to the computer she pointed at. "I honestly didn't know she worked here," he said, embarrassed.

"I'm surprised she's legal enough to work at all," Mandy said, giving him an equal scowl. "You told me you aren't seeing anyone else."

"I'm not, I swear, and for the record, she's twenty-one. I was with her months ago, before we started—" He didn't finish his sentence. He sat in the chair in front of the computer and reached out for another chair nearby, rolling it up beside him. The computer screen lit up and asked for a code. "Ah, hell," James said. "Can you go to the counter and get the code to access the computer?" Mandy, still reeling over the counter girl, didn't respond. "Fine. I'll get it, even though I'm trying to help you." He stood up and looked down at Mandy. "You weren't a nun before you met me, you know."

Mandy laughed with an angry smile. "I know. I was with your brother."

James sighed and went to the counter. Mandy looked at the computer screen blankly. Why was she upset? James had a reputation. She knew it before getting involved with him.

James sat back down at the computer. Mandy reached out under the desk and grabbed his hand. "Thank you for helping me today," she said. "And for coming over last night. I needed it."

James gave her a smirk as he typed in the access code. "It's okay." He clicked on an icon on the desktop and clicked on a button that read 'connect.' The computer made multiple screeching sounds, and Mandy looked at him confused.

"You can't tell me you never been online before?" he said with a laugh. "It's just connecting to the net." It took what felt like forever for the red light to turn green, and finally, a notification read 'connected.'

James clicked on another icon, opening up a browser. "Okay, I can start searching online for information."

"So you just type in anything, and the computer looks it up?"

"You sound like an old lady! It's 1994 now, Mandy. Get with the times. Yes. You type in whatever you want, and it will search online for anything related to what we asked for it to search for."

"Type in Callie Knox," she said hopefully.

He typed in her name, but the page was empty. "Zero results."

"Let's try Steph Moore." James typed in the name, and the page lit up with multiple articles.

"We got something?" Mandy asked.

"Not exactly," James said with a smile. "This is all for an actor named Michael Moore. Sometimes, the web will give you things that are more relevant to the entire world. More prevalent articles will be put at the top of the page. This search gave us" — he looked at the top corner of the browser— "over a hundred thousand pages to review. That won't work, but I think I know how we can narrow this down." He typed in the word 'Steph,' then hit the plus sign on the keyboard, then typed 'Moore,' another plus, and then 'Cranston.' Finally, he hit enter.

Mandy looked at the top corner of the browser and noticed again that there were over ten thousand articles this time. "I guess that's not much better." She looked at the first few articles, but none of them had the name Steph Moore in it. She felt even more confused.

"It is though," he said. "Read the headlines of the articles. That's our county."

Mandy took a moment to read the full article title. 'Essex County Man, Ryland Moore, Charged with Double Homicide.' She grabbed the mouse from James and clicked on the article. Her eyes raced across each line, taking in the information.

A local man from Essex County, Ryland Moore, has been charged with the murders of Theresa and Karen Hardwauld. The teen-aged women's bodies were found in a wooded area of Essex County late Thursday night.

Mandy looked at the date the article was printed and was amazed it was only five years ago. She continued to read.

Detective Alda Lane from the Pennsylvania state police major crimes unit was asked by reporters if the crimes are related to several other murders across the state, all of young women found deceased in the woods, however she was not able to comment at this time.

"Would you look at that?" James said when he read the detective's name. In the article was a picture of Detective Lane beside a reporter. When she first met her, the detective had come across almost macho, wearing an oversized trench coat and with short hair, but in this older photo of her, she looked more feminine. She wore a pants suit and had long, curly hair.

"She looked much better with longer hair," James said to himself.

James clicked out of the article and went to another one that was titled, 'Serial Killer Ryland Moore Convicted with Six Counts of First-Degree Murder.'

Local Essex County resident Ryland Moore has been convicted of six murders in connection with the Hardwauld sisters. Judge Tren-

ton Valums ruled a sentence of a hundred and fifty years in prison, without the possibility of parole.

Ryland Moore has been convicted of murdering several teenage girls, as young as thirteen. All the girls' bodies were found in different areas of the state, but several within Essex County. All deceased were discovered in the woods, their bodies unclothed. The police have confirmed that all women were brutally beaten and sexually abused before their deaths, at the hands of Mr. Moore.

Mandy saw in the article a picture of a large woman in front of a water tower that read 'Lance.' The caption below read, 'Wife of Serial Killer Proclaims His Innocence.'

Reporters asked Mrs. Patricia Moore, at her house, what she thought of the judge's sentence of her husband. "He didn't do it, period." Mrs. Moore would not comment further.

"I know that town," James said, pointing at the water tower. "I know exactly where she lives."

Mandy nodded her head. "Have time for a road trip?"

CHAPTER ELEVEN

Mandy smiled when they drove up to the house of Patricia Moore. Behind the small home was the water tower they'd seen in the article. She kissed James on the lips before she got out.

Mandy knocked gently on the door. She looked for a doorbell but couldn't find one. A 'no soliciting' sticker was below the doorknob and another on the mailbox beside the door.

"You need to knock a little louder than that if you want someone's attention," James said, banging on the door until he heard movement inside.

Patricia Moore opened the door. She looked like she had gained much more weight since the picture from the article had been taken. A cigarette was loosely hanging off her lips.

"Who are you?" she asked with a harsh tone.

Mandy cleared her throat. "I'm sorry to bother you, but apparently my daughter and yours are friends. My girl, Callie? She's missing."

"Callie?" the woman asked confused. "You mean Cas?"

Mandy felt her heart beat faster. She grabbed a picture out of her purse and presented it to Patricia. "This is my daughter, Callie Knox. I'm her mother. The police tell me she is friends with your daughter, Steph."

"Well Ms. Knox, I know this young woman very well, but she's always called herself Cas to me. And call me Pat."

Mandy felt her chest tighten a moment. Her daughter had been calling herself by a different name as well.

"Do you know where your daughter is?" asked James.

Pat laughed. "No, but she'll come back. She always does. I can't believe she took Cas with her. I mean, Callie, right?" Mandy nodded her head. "Would you like to come in for some tea?"

"Thanks," James said, holding the door open for Mandy and Pat. They walked inside her small home. In the narrow room was her kitchen and living room, side by side. Pat gestured for them to sit at a small table.

"I only have pekoe tea," she said to them.

"A little milk in it for me," James said.

Pat smiled, looking at Mandy, "I always wondered who Ca— Callie's parents were. She seems like such a good girl. Not like my daughter."

"James is her uncle," Mandy corrected. "So my daughter and yours are good friends?" Mandy asked.

"I don't understand it either," Pat said with a laugh. "What an odd couple those two are."

"And Steph has run away before?" James asked.

Pat took out two mugs from a cupboard and took a kettle off the stove. "Oh yeah, many times. She eventually makes her way back here, whenever she's stuck somewhere or needs money." She poured the hot water in the mugs and tossed a teabag in both.

"Where do you think they went?" Mandy asked.

Pat placed a mug in front of her and then one before James. "Oh, wherever she can spread her legs for a few bucks, I'm sure." She caught herself again. "Not to say that your Callie would do that. Like I said, she's a good girl. She just found herself with a bad crowd, mainly Steph." Pat grabbed a mug she had on the counter, taking a sip. "Your daughter will be okay. Whenever I hear from Steph, I'll let you know. Just leave me your number."

"How do they even know each other?" James asked. "Wouldn't your daughter be at the local high school in town?"

"She did go there," Pat said. "That was until they caught her doing drugs under the bleachers at lunch. It wasn't her first time, but it was the last suspension. They kicked her out. Cranston High was the only one that would take her. I guess they must have met at school."

"How did she even get to school? It's an hour drive," James said, confused.

"That was her problem," Pat answered sharply. "I told her though, if she can't pass high school, she needs to get her skinny ass out of my house or pay me rent."

"Did my daughter have a boyfriend that you knew of?" Mandy asked.

"No, I never met anyone or heard of them talking about one." Pat took another sip of her tea.

"What about your daughter?" James asked her.

Pat laughed. "Only for nights at a time." She looked at Mandy with a stunned look. "You must think I'm wicked talking about my own daughter like that. You don't know what it's like. Your daughter is an angel compared to my Steph. There's only so much I can do about how she is. She does whatever she wants, whenever she wants. She's over eighteen now. I can't stop her."

"The police asked me if my daughter had any kind of a blog," Mandy said. "I didn't know of any, but did Steph?"

Pat put down her mug. "Don't get me started on that stupid blog. I swear, the way she puts down her own family on it, for the whole world to read, amazes me."

"Can we read it?" James asked. "We're hoping to see if it will help us figure out where Callie is."

Pat nodded her head. "Anybody can read it. The whole world can. She made me read a journal or blog or whatever you call it once. Disgusted me. I think she did it just to spite me. She shamed her father. I almost threw her out of the house. She was lucky she was only seventeen at the time, or I would have." Pat rolled her eyes up. "What the hell was the name of it? The site was called E-Journal, and her nickname was DarkQueen1975."

"Thanks, Pat," Mandy said.

"Your husband," James said, "he was charged with those murders?" Mandy looked at him, amazed that he had brought it up. They'd decided on the ride over that they wouldn't bring up the matter since it had nothing to do with Callie.

"It's a bunch of bullshit!" Pat said raising her voice. "He wouldn't have killed those girls. He's not that kind of man. They had no evidence on him at all! The police made a big fuss that he was a truck driver. He travelled to some of those areas where those girls went missing. So what though?"

"What about the hairclip they found in the back of his truck?" James asked. "Police linked it to one of those girls, right?" Mandy was enraged inside but kept a cool demeaner. She didn't even remember seeing anything about a hairclip in the articles they'd read.

"No!" Pat barked. "That could have been anyone's. I mean, it wasn't his, obviously. Ryland, he was a complicated husband. He liked to pick up girls on his route for...well, you know. He would be gone for days. I sat at home, thinking he missed me like an asshole, while he was out there doing whatever he felt like. He fessed up to me about it after he was arrested. Obviously, Steph got his personality." Pat laughed. "Even in prison, that man finds a way to cheat. Did you know they can have pen pals in prison? Girls will actually write to people like Ryland, wanting to meet him for sex. I found out and stopped seeing him. He's convicted of murdering young girls, and these women actually want him still? Makes me sick. I stopped seeing him and forbade Steph too."

"But you still think he didn't do it?" James asked.

"That's right. He's a two-timing piece of shit, but not a murderer." Pat took a deep breath, reaching for her mug, and took a large sip.

"I'm sorry if we upset you, Pat," Mandy said, cutting James off before he could ask another stupid question. "I wanted to meet you and hopefully figure out where Callie is, or at least get a better idea."

Pat nodded her head. "I understand. The first time Steph ran, I was a wreck for a few days. You'll get used to it."

CHAPTER TWELVE

James drove to his home. It was closer than Cyber Café, and Mandy wanted answers right away. The last thing she could handle was waiting any more to read Steph's blog. Typically, Mandy would never drive with James to his house during the day like this, but she didn't care anymore. James' property was larger, anyway. There were only a few neighbors on the block who would have noticed, but James said he never really spoke to them, so he was never too concerned about them seeing Mandy. It was Mandy who demanded they meet at a motel room.

Mandy walked into the large home, shutting the door behind her. It always shook her how beautiful his house was. A large fireplace, with brick going up the great room's large ceilings, took her breath away. The nearby kitchen was huge, and even had a built-in fridge that was made to look like it was part of the many cabinets.

James grabbed her hand and led her to his office upstairs, passing his large bedroom. James grabbed a second chair for Mandy and sat in front of his television sized computer screen.

"Take a seat," he said to Mandy, patting the chair. Mandy had never been inside his office before. On the wall was a few degrees that James had achieved. One of them was his master's in business and technology degree. It amazed her how successful he was compared to his brother.

"Is your boss upset you took the day off?" Mandy asked.

James laughed. "You know me. I'm basically my own boss

there. They are lucky they have me at all in this market. That's why I'm telling you I don't have to travel anymore, if you don't want me to. I can stay here with you."

"Steve would a problem, I think," Mandy said. She wasn't sure why she had even mentioned his name. She tried her best to never bring him up when they were together.

"I'll deal with my brother someday," he said curtly. "I'm just logging online again." The computer made more screeching sounds, and it felt like it was taking even longer than last time to connect to the net.

When he finally did, he opened up a browser and was able to find the website E-Journal quickly. He typed in the words 'Dark-Bitch1975.'

"No, it's DarkQueen1975," Mandy corrected.

"Right," James said, typing in the proper username. A picture of Steph Moore popped up on the site, and next it were the words, 'Read my life, if you dare.'

James scrolled down the online journal. He stopped on a few pictures of Steph dressed in just a dark bra. Steph was lying in a bed, her back arched and her arms stretched out. Mandy assumed she'd taken the picture herself from the angle. From the bareness of her skin around her hips, Mandy figured she wasn't wearing panties, but the picture ended right at her pelvis line.

"This girl is something else," James said, shaking his head. "I can't believe Callie is friends with her."

I can't believe anything anymore, Mandy thought.

The title of the blog caught her attention. 'How to Fuck Your Teacher to Get an A.' James leaned in and began reading.

"I can't do this," Mandy said. "I'm not going to read this girl's sex journal. I just want to know if Callie is in it somewhere, that's it."

James nodded. "Easy enough." He hit the Control key on the keyboard and then the letter F. A search bar opened up. "Since all the blogs are on one page, I can search to see if Callie's name is anywhere on it." He typed in 'Callie,' but zero results were found. Mandy looked at him, and he nodded his head. "Right, she goes by

'Cas' now."

A blog near the end of the page was highlighted. 'Partners In Crime,' the headline read. Below the title was a picture of Steph, with her large tongue sticking out and her middle finger up. Beside her was Callie. She wore a large smile in the picture, her own middle finger pointed sideways.

"You okay?" James asked.

Mandy nodded her head and started reading the post.

These two creeps are out of this shit town. Hollywood? L.A.? Who cares? Anywhere but here. We made a pledge. Wherever we go, we will do it together. This world is shit, but when we're together, it's less smelly.

For my fan boys out there, keep reading. When we figure out our shit, I want to meet you too someday, mostly because we will be homeless ;)

The short blog ended there.

"When was this posted?" Mandy asked.

James scrolled up. "Last week. This was the last post too. We will have to keep coming back to this site until she posts again. I'm sure she will say which city she ends up in. Maybe we get lucky and she takes a picture of some kind of landmark. We can call the police there and ask for help, or hell, grab a flight and go there." James stood up from the computer chair. "As much as you hate it, I think we should read her other blogs on here." Mandy nodded her head in agreement. "But first, I need a beer. You?" Mandy looked at him, and James covered his mouth. "I didn't mean anything by that, sorry. I don't know what I was thinking. I wasn't thinking. I don't need one, really."

"It's okay, James." Mandy was pissed inside though. Of course. she wanted to drink. She always wanted a drink. Until the moment she died, she would want a drink, but she chose not to go down that path again. She knew where it could bring her. For a moment, she thought of the gun hidden in her bedroom. "If you want a beer though, you can. You don't have to hide it from me, I've told you that.

"No, I'm good, I mean it," James said. "Take my chair, you

can scroll where you want."

"Thanks," Mandy said, moving over to the chair in front of the computer. She scrolled up to the picture of Callie again. She could feel a tear forming. The smile on her daughter's face was genuine.

Wherever she is, maybe she's at least happy, she thought. She looked at the picture again, this time noticing the arms in the picture. One of Steph's hands was giving the middle finger, while the other arm was wrapped around Callie's shoulder. One of Callie's arms was at her side, while the other gave the finger too. There was another hand though, wrapped around Callie's waist, but it was from someone outside of the picture.

She pointed it out to James. "I need to know whose hand that is," she said, determined.

She scrolled all the way to the top, past the revealing photos of Steph again. "The first blog was from last year. Maybe there's more of Callie, or maybe some name of a guy she likes. Anything. There has to be more."

"We could visit my parents old place, like I said before. Get away from all of this for a day or so. I never disconnected my mom's internet either. We could go right now, just us."

Mandy looked at him and back at the screen. Why would he want to bring her there? She hated her mother-in-law. She couldn't stand that overbearing woman. She'd always tried to tell Mandy how to raise her daughter, as if she were mom of the year. She ignored James and started reading.

James rubbed her back. "We can take as long as we need tonight and read everything." His hand fell to her lap, caressing her thighs.

Mandy was so deep into a blog post that she didn't notice his touch. James slipped his hand between her thighs and reached down, taking his time feeling her mound over her jeans.

Mandy flinched. "James! Stop!"

James didn't move his hand as commanded. "What's wrong?"

Mandy looked down at his hand, then back at the computer

screen, where a scantily clad Steph Moore looked back at her. "What's wrong with you?" She stood up, and James' hand lay limp on the chair where she once sat.

"Sorry, I misread you," James said. "Let's just read—"

Mandy raised her arms. "No, I'm good for tonight. I'll let you do whatever you want while you read her journals by yourself."

Mandy stormed out of the office and headed down the stairs, while James shouted for her to come back.

CHAPTER THIRTEEN

Mandy took a taxi home. She stopped at the Cyber Café nearby first, but ran back to the taxi when she saw the closed sign in the front door. She might not have been able to look more into Steph's blog, but she had more than enough to follow up on.

Whose arm was around Callie's hip?

Once inside her home, she headed right for the phone book again. She opened up the white pages until she found the last name she was looking for—Peterson. She said a silent prayer as she looked for the drama teacher's name, hoping he wasn't unlisted.

Randall Peterson. 11462 County Road 4. She smiled when she saw his number. Mandy was surprised he lived somewhere outside of Cranston. She didn't picture the drama teacher as someone who enjoyed country living. With his bright clothing, she pictured him more of a city slicker.

She dialed his number and waited anxiously for someone to pick up.

"Hello?" he answered after a few rings. "Peterson residence."

"Mr. Peterson? Sorry, Rand" Mandy said. "It's Ms. Knox."

"How are you doing? All the staff have been thinking of you and Callie."

"Thanks," she said, and meant it. "It's been a difficult few days."

"I heard on the news that her case is now considered a missing persons?"

Mandy sighed. She never even thought about the news. She didn't even think about turning on the television to watch her daughter's face plastered over the six o'clock news. She used to watch the anchors vomit out each terrible story of the dead and tragically injured, thinking how horrible it must be to for them and their families, but then go about her day without a care.

Now here she was, her daughter part of the news. She thought about others thinking how poor old Amanda Knox is doing and then going back to eating their dinner or playing with their children or anything but worrying any further about what had happened to her daughter.

"It has, yes," Mandy answered. "I'm trying to understand what's been going on with Callie. I met the mother of one of her friends, Steph Moore. She's missing too. Do you know Steph?"

He cleared his throat. "Only by reputation. I've never taught her. She is a troubled youth from what I know. I didn't know her and Callie knew each other."

Me too, Mandy thought.

"The police think that they may be together somewhere, but they are still looking into things." Mandy looked down, fighting off the urge to cry. "Listen, I saw a picture of Callie, and it looked like some boy's hand was wrapped around her. Did you know if she had a boyfriend or any boy she was talking to?"

"I'm sorry, Ms. Knox, I don't," he said curtly. "I try to just teach the children and stay out of whatever *drama* they stir up amongst themselves."

"Besides Steph, was there maybe another friend who may know? I remember she did talk to a girl named Jess, I think it was? Jessica—"

"Summers?" the teacher said. "I got the idea that those two weren't really close now."

"Do you know why?"

"Like I said, I try and stay out of their drama so I can teach drama," he said with a laugh. "They were close at one point, when Jessica was Callie's understudy for Juliette in the play."

"I forgot about that," Mandy said with enthusiasm. "Why did you get the impression that they weren't friends?"

The drama teacher cleared his throat again. "I'm really not sure what to say. I heard Jessica calling your daughter a bad word when talking with other girls in the auditorium."

"What did she call her?"

"I'm not sure that matters—"

"Please, Mr. Peterson," Mandy pleaded. "What was it?"

"White trash slut. You know how these kids are, Ms. Knox. We were both in high school at some point. They can be mean and say stupid things. Listen, I have company coming by soon, and I should really go."

"I'm so sorry I just called you like this, Mr. Peterson. I hope I wasn't bothering you."

"No, Ms. Knox. I understand. This must be truly tough for you."

Mandy still had more questions, though, and couldn't stop talking until she got more answers. "Did my daughter ever talk to you or the other girls about moving somewhere, or being an actress in Hollywood?"

Mr. Peterson laughed. "Of course. They all do though. Callie was one of the few that I thought could make it, though. I just wish she'd stuck it out in drama for her last semester. Just so you know, some of us are talking to Principal Blacksmith about giving her an honorary degree for the hard work she put into school, besides the last semester. I'll let you know if something comes out of that."

"Thanks," Mandy said.

"I already spoke to Detective Lane and that tall, scary looking man too."

"Detective Ferguson."

"That's the one," he said, laughing. "Who wants to be a bad guy when cops like him exist?"

"Well, I'm sorry I bothered you. Thanks for taking some time and talking to me."

"No, anytime," he said. "Don't hesitate to call or come by."

Mandy thanked him again before ending the phone call. She didn't feel much further in understanding what had happened to Callie, but knew a boy was involved in this in some way. Something told her that Jessica Summers knew something about that boy. Girls didn't go calling other girls white trash sluts for no reason other than boys.

Mandy looked through the phone book again until she found an address.

Two weeks before missing.

Jessica Summers.

Add her to the list of people I can't wait to never see again.

Mr. Peterson says that when trying to act out a character, it's important to understand their central drive and flaw.

Jessica's was an easy one to find. What was her central flaw? Jealousy. What drove her? To be the one other people would be jealous of.

When I got lead in the school play as Juliette, she was my understudy. She didn't have to tell me out loud for me to know what she truly felt. I could see in her eyes, when we practiced our lines together, that she held out hope for me to magically get sick on the night of the play or get hit by a car or just disappear, so that she could shine.

I was entirely unaware of the kind of girl Jessica Summers was.

What she did, I'll never forget.

I got revenge though. I made sure she would never forget either.

When I'm gone and I've made it, I will love the sensation I have each day, knowing somewhere in the little town of Cranston, Jessica Summers' jealousy is in overdrive.

CHAPTER FOURTEEN

Mandy knocked on another Summers' residence front door. This was the third address in the phone book with the last name Summers. For a small town, there were five separate addresses. The first two she'd visited didn't know a young girl named Jessica. Unfortunately, the white pages didn't exactly break down addresses by eighteen-year-old girls.

The door opened, and Mandy smiled at the change of her luck.

"Hey, Jessica," Mandy said to the young woman.

Jessica leaned against her front door with an arched eyebrow. She shoved her brown hair to one side, fixing her pink summer dress.

"Ms. Knox?" she asked. "What are you doing here?"

"I was actually hoping to talk to you about Callie." Mandy tried her best at hiding her enthusiasm for seeing her after two failed attempts.

"I heard about it at school, of course," she said, "but I don't really—"

"Does she have a boyfriend? I'm trying to figure out who she was talking to."

Jessica sighed. "I'm just not comfortable, really. I—"

Mandy took a step forward. As she did, Jessica tensed. "Are your parents home?"

Jessica looked inside her home, then back at her. "No, but I'd like if you—"

"I could come back when they are home," Mandy said. "I

need to know what was happening with my daughter, and I feel like you know, at least more than I do." Jessica stared at her awkwardly, attempting to find words to shoo the woman away, Mandy assumed. "Let's start with Steph Moore, do you know her?"

"That slut—" Jessica stopped herself. "Sorry."

"That's okay." She wondered if Jessica had ever read Steph's blog. "Was she and my daughter hanging out a lot?"

"Yeah. Always by the bleachers. It was their *spot*. A lot of us, even the teachers, knew what she did there."

"Drugs, right?"

Jessica nodded her head. "That's right."

"Steph had a reputation too, from what I heard. Sounds like she was with men, some older. I heard one was a teacher."

"No fucking way!" Jessica said with enthusiasm. "Did Callie tell you that? We heard the stories, but none of us believed it. It has to be true."

Mandy took in a breath. There was a time in her life where she likely would have connected well with a girl like Jessica. She'd been the pretty queen bee of the high school. Mandy hated the thought that if she were in high school, she would be one of those girls making fun of a girl like Steph Moore, or worse, Callie.

"Which teacher did you hear she slept with?" she asked the young girl. She almost felt like she was in high school exchanging gossip again.

Jessica looked at her with thin lips. "Listen, I'm not sure I should be telling a—"

"Come on! Don't you remember that one time you slept over? I ordered pizza, and we watched that movie all together."

"That wasn't me, Ms. Knox."

Mandy sighed. "I heard Mr. Peterson was the one she slept with," she lied.

Jessica scrunched her face in disgust. "What? That faggot, no way." Mandy kept her cool. She'd forgotten how cruel kids could be when talking about people. "I heard it was Mr. Greyson," Jessica continued.

Mandy would look into that further, and she should even

report it to Detective Lane. *What a scumbag.* Steph was likely seventeen at the time. Mandy reminded herself that it was only a rumor.

"Did my daughter ever talk about running away somewhere? Hollywood, or New York, or some big city?"

"Hollywood mostly. She didn't talk about running away though. She wanted to go to college, I think." That was the Callie that she remembered too. "But she kept gloating about how some talent agent guy was interested in her. She told anybody who would listen about how much of a big of a star she was going to be."

"So you think she just left because this talent agent was encouraging her?" Jessica shrugged her shoulders. "Do you have their name? The talent agent?" Jessica shook her head no. "Now, about the possible boy she was seeing," Mandy continued. "Any idea who it was?"

Jessica rolled her eyes. "It's getting real late now—"

"White trash slut," Mandy blurted out. Jessica stopped talking. "I heard that's what you called my daughter. Now, call me crazy, but there's a reason you would call her that. It was probably because of a boy. She must have been seeing someone, maybe someone you liked even."

"Fine! It was Fin, okay? I dated him for a bit, and Callie just hooked up with him! Happy?"

Mandy was, but she didn't let her know. "What's Fin's last name?"

"Fin Lentz."

"Does Fin have a car? Do you think he drove my daughter somewhere?"

Steph laughed. "No way. He dumped her. He's still in town as we speak."

"Where can I find him on a night like this?"

Jessica smiled. "He's working."

"Where?"

CHAPTER FIFTEEN

Ace High Club.

Every small town had their dive bars. This was Cranston's. She had been here many times before. How many nights had she blacked out at the bar, waiting for the bartender to save her from men with erections wanting to prey on her? Sometimes, she voluntarily went home with them.

It was a different time, she reminded herself. She was a new woman.

What do I have left though? she wondered as she walked through the saloon style doors of the Ace High Club. *Callie is gone. All I have is my train wreck of a life.*

It had been over a year since she was inside the bar, and it looked just as she remembered. The black bear head still hung over the bar. Her shoes still slightly stuck to the floor with each step she took inside. The tables, chairs, and furniture were in need of some type of repair. She didn't even want to go visit the bathrooms again to see if the one toilet was still out of order, but she assumed it was.

The darkly lit room showed a few patrons drinking, mostly by themselves. A part of her missed that sense of isolation she had here. The dark room made it easy to forget you were part of the world, and you could drink your sorrows away with no concern. Worse, the smell of beer hit her nostrils hard.

Behind the bar, a young man lifted a beer case onto the counter. When he did, his bicep muscles almost ripped out of his tight white shirt. He opened the beer case and started shoving them one by one inside a minifridge behind him. He stopped a moment, taking a white towel off his shoulder to wipe his forehead.

As Mandy walked closer to the young man, who she assumed was Fin Lentz, the bartender stopped and stared at her, taking his time to look at Mandy's physique.

"What can I get you?" he asked her.

"I was hoping to talk to you. You're Fin, right?"

"Must be my lucky day," Fin said with a smile. "You're a bit older than me, but love is blind."

Mandy wanted to puke. This was the boy Callie had been seeing? Sure, he was handsome, but in a slithery, dirty way.

"I'm Mandy Knox, Callie's mom," she said. "Although I guess she goes by Cas now."

Fin looked at her again, taking his time to let Mandy know he was checking her out. "I definitely see the resemblance now."

"Do you know where she is?"

"Cas? No clue." A man barely managed to walk up to the bar, waving for Fin's attention. Fin nodded his head but pointed two fingers in the air, then he took out two shot glasses from a shelf behind him, pouring whiskey to the top in both.

"I heard you two were seeing each other," Mandy started, but Fin shrugged at her. "Do you know Steph Moore too?" He smiled and shrugged again. Mandy took a deep breath. "You know, I can ask the police to just ask you questions if you prefer?"

"Detective Lane and Ferguson?" Fin said with a devilish smile. "Already spoke to them." Mandy breathed out. Why hadn't Detective Lane told her she knew Callie was seeing a guy? "Listen," Fin said with a smirk, "I'll tell you what I told them, but first..." He pushed the two shot glasses towards her. "We drink."

"No," Mandy said. "Stop playing games. Just tell me now!"

Fin shook his head, brushing his hair to one side. "You heard me. Drink, or get out of the bar. No loitering around here." Mandy grabbed the shot glass and downed it without thinking. Fin grabbed the other and drank it, slamming the glass on the counter.

The old man on the other side of the bar yelled out, "Whoa!" and laughed to himself.

Fin smiled again. "I thought I heard something about you being sober. Pretty sure Cas told me that."

"Now you know my daughter?" Mandy asked, unamused.

"Of course we hooked up." Fin went to the other side of the bar, grabbing a few beers for the old man. Mandy walked to the other side, following him.

"How long were you sober for?" Fin asked. "I guess you're going to have to bring back your sober badge, or sticker, or whatever they give you."

"My daughter?" Mandy reminded him. "Where is she?"

"You already know," Fin says. "Jessica called me before you came. She told you."

"Hollywood?"

"Most likely." Fin took towel off his shoulder, wiping down the counter. "Yes, they wanted me to drive them, but I had enough of those bitches." Fin looked at Mandy. "I was mostly talking about Steph. I haven't seen them in a while."

"Why now? Why did they just leave?" Mandy asked. She could taste the sweetness of the whiskey in her mouth. She wanted more. She could grab the bottle from Fin and down it easily, but she tried to stay focused.

She'd slipped. It happened. She could get back on the right path immediately. *Never say you're going to do better tomorrow. That's just an excuse to do whatever you want today.* That was what the substance abuse workers had told her at High River Hospital.

Fin laughed. "There was this talent agent guy. A few weeks before she left, we were sitting in the alley out back. I grabbed some *supply* from the bar, and the three of us had a good time."

"What?"

"Cas, Steph, and me. We would drink in the alley. My boss lets me get away with shit like that, since I bring in some of the local women, who in turn, bring in the lonely men. I have a talent, I guess. That night though, some guy, who I've seen in the bar a few times, comes up to the three of us, enamored with Cas. Tells her she's the most beautiful woman he's ever seen. Gives her some card and tells us he's a talent agent. He mostly works on finding extras for local projects but has some connections in Hollywood. Says he could help us."

"'Us'?"

"Well, of course he gave me a card too."

"What was his name?"

"Honestly, it happened a few weeks, ago. I tossed his card. I didn't pay it much mind. Cas, though, was different. She wanted to meet up with the guy. That girl has a goal, and nothing will get in her way.

"How long did you see Cas for?" Mandy asked.

"Like I said, it was nothing serious. We just hooked up a few times."

"I take it Jessica was mad about that?" Mandy asked.

"That girl is worse. Thinks I'm hers. I told her today when she called, I do whatever I want, to whomever I want." Fin stared at Mandy. It wasn't hard to see what he was thinking. Mandy tried to maintain her anger at the boy. "I told the cops about this guy too." Mandy felt more anger at the lack of information Detective Lane was sharing with her. She could be helping them find out where her daughter was.

Fin grabbed two more shot glasses, filling them with whiskey again. "Another?" he asked with a wicked smile. "On me. I'm off in an hour too, if you want to stick around."

"To get drunk in the alley with you?" Mandy said mockingly. She stood up from the bar stool. She tried to control herself before she said something that she would regret. "If you hear anything about my daughter, I'm guessing you know where I live?" Fin nodded his head.

"No problem," Fin said. He downed the two shots easily. "I know where to find you."

One week before missing.

At what point did I become the parent?

My mom is the worst. She always has some new drama that's erupting in her life. She pretends that she doesn't like it, but she does. Without the drama, she would just be a boring waitress, with nothing else going on.

I made the mistake of telling Dad that I was thinking about moving right to Los Angeles instead of going to college. He got heated. The look in his eyes sometimes scares me. I honestly feel like he would kill me if I did leave. He reminded me that all the hours he puts in his truck is to give me a good life, and that I would waste it with my pipe dream.

"Then how about letting me live my life?"

I thought he was going to hit me when I said that to him.

I took off though. Fin picked me up a few blocks away at a gas station.

At some point, I thought I'd found love in Cranston with Fin. How dumb was I?

When I thanked Fin for picking me up, he only had one thing on his mind—for me to show him how grateful I was. I shot him down this time.

I don't need small-town Cranston love. I'm no longer bound by my parents. My mom needs to live her life, my father can't control mine, and I need to live my own.

CHAPTER SIXTEEN

Mandy sat on her living room couch, staring at the ceiling, wondering what to do next. Detective Lane's card was on the kitchen counter. She looked at the clock and saw it was now past midnight. She would call her tomorrow. She also wanted to go back to the Cyber Café, to read more into Steph Moore blog posts. She wasn't sure what else she could find out from them but figured it couldn't hurt.

What's the point? She's gone. If she wants to come back home, she will, someday.

She thought of Pat Moore. *"You'll get used to this,"* she has said to her. She didn't think she had that kind of relationship with her daughter though. Was she so blind to what she had with Callie?

Mandy could feel something rotten in her stomach. It could have been the alcohol, but it wasn't. Since coming home from the bar, she'd fought the urge to drink more. She could easily go to a late-night liquor store and quench her thirst. She knew better than to do that.

She had picked up the phone once or twice to call James. When she didn't think about drinking, she thought about being with him, but she also knew better than to call him. She was still mad over what had happened.

Mandy walked up stairs and opened Callie's bedroom. The police had told her that they hadn't found a journal. She wondered how hard they'd looked, after all, they didn't find her gun. Maybe the police had found the gun but didn't mention it to her. She had a legal permit for it.

She looked under Callie's bed, wondering how dumb she could be for thinking it would just be lying there among the dust bunnies. She felt under the bed mattress and looked in drawers. She opened the closet, pushing dresses, skirts, and shirts from side to side.

She knew she wouldn't find one. She knew Callie didn't keep a journal. That seemed to be the only thing she actually had right about her daughter.

It made her uneasy when she thought about what Callie's journal would say about her if she did have one. *The drunk mother?* The train wreck of a life Mandy had. Of course she would want to get away from Mandy. Who wouldn't?

Mandy could feel a tear forming as she sat on her knees, searching through boxes at the bottom of her daughter's closet. She felt that sickness inside her again. It felt almost painful. It was what she imagined people with cancer felt when the blackness took over their insides.

Callie didn't run away. No, she didn't. She would have left a note or called. Something is wrong.

The phone began to ring, and Mandy stood up, almost losing her balance.

This isn't right. None of it is. The pig's blood. Steph Moore. Fin.

Suddenly, the sickness she felt in her stomach crawled up her throat. She had a brief moment to turn her head and move her hair out of the way as she vomitted. The phone continued to ring downstairs. Mandy wiped her mouth and took her time going to the kitchen.

The answering machine turned on. "Hey, it's me," James said into the machine. "Are you awake? Pick up if you are. Can we talk?" Mandy managed to get inside her kitchen when James said, "Okay, just call me back when you get this."

Mandy picked up the phone, but James had already disconnected. She hung up the phone and picked up the receiver, dialing his number.

Suddenly a noise at the front door startled her. She heard

loud thumps, and finally, the turn of her locked door. The front door opened with a loud creak, and her ex-husband stormed into the room with a grimace.

"Where is she?" he demanded. She could already tell he was drunk. He took a few more steps towards her, and his stench confirmed it.

Mandy picked up the phone and dialed nine, then one. She looked at him. "Stop, don't come closer to me, Steve!"

"I just got back in town. Where is my daughter, bitch?"

"I don't know. The police are looking—"

"What have you been doing?" he asked condescendingly.

"More than you," she barked back.

"I'd cut that out," he said swiftly. "It's been a long night, so tell me everything, now."

Mandy took a deep beath. He had a right to know what she'd found out. She told Steve about the pig's blood, her talking to people from school, and Jessica and Fin.

"My girl is seeing a bartender?" he said with a sigh. He looked at Mandy with his beady eyes. "Did you go there tonight? I smell liquor on you."

"That's just you," Mandy said.

Steve smiled, but when he did, it made him look uglier. "Ever since we broke it off, you seem to think I'm some limp noodle who will take your lip. I'm not. Tread lightly. I'm trying to fix this mess you made."

"What?"

"She left because of you!"

"It sounds like she planned this out!" Mandy yelled back. "Some talent agent told her she had what it takes to make it. She has some friend, Steph Moore, she's with Callie."

"Moore?"

"Yeah. She's the daughter of some guy named Ryland Moore."

"The serial killer?"

Mandy nodded her head. "She goes from being perfect to dropping out of school and hanging out with girls like Steph

Moore. I don't get it."

Steve pounded his large fist into a wall, leaving a mark. He turned and started to walk towards the front door.

"Where are you going?" Mandy asked.

"To fix this mess you made," Steve said, slamming the door behind him.

Two days before missing.

Thelma and Louise.
That's what Steph is to me.
I hate myself for thinking poorly about her at first.
All people see is the shell she puts out to the world.
Nobody understands what's inside, what really makes her, her.
I do now.
Mr. Greyson, that slimeball, did only one thing worthwhile in his life when he paired us together for a class project. We hung out a few times, and I finally got to know who she really was.
I thought I had it bad. Her dad literally killed people. He's rotting in prison somewhere. She hasn't spoken to him in years. Even before that, she never really knew her father well. He was a trucker, just like my dad.
She's just so different than girls like Jessica. She doesn't judge me. She listens.
Steph makes the most boring days more fun, just by being herself. She's a walking one-woman party.
Things got rocky with us when she told me Fin tried to hook up with her one night. She told him off and came to me with everything.
Don't get made, she told me. We need his car.
We have a plan now. Perfect timing. Jessica found out about Fin and me. She's making life hell for me at school. Steph had an easy answer for that too. Fuck school. Don't show up. Sign yourself out of school, you're eighteen now.
Two more days.
Sayonara, Cranston and everyone in it.

CHAPTER SEVENTEEN

Mandy barely slept. As soon as her clock said it was past eight in the morning, she jumped out of bed and ran to her kitchen phone. She grabbed Detective Lane's card and entered in her number. She didn't pick up, but Mandy left a message for her to return her call.

She sat impatiently at her kitchen table. She picked up the phone and dialed 911. A woman answered almost right away. "911. What's your emergency?"

"Sorry. My name is Amanda Knox. I'm trying to get a hold of Detective Alda Lane with the state police."

"Is this some kind of emergency?" the operator asked.

Mandy took a breath. "No, it's not. I—"

"I'll give the number for the state police. You can ask to speak to the detective. Please don't call 911 if it's not an emergency, ma'am."

Mandy apologized and wrote the number for the station. When she called, she asked the new operator to speak to Detective Lane.

"I'm sorry, but she's not available. Is this for an active case?" the operator asked.

"Yes, for Callie Knox," Mandy said.

"Well, her partner, Detective Ferguson, is here today. I can put you through."

Mandy thanked the operator, and she connected her to Detective Ferguson's line.

"Detective Ferguson here," he answered after a few rings.

"Who is calling?"

"This is Mandy Knox," she said.

"Yes, hi, Ms. Knox," Detective Ferguson said. "How are you doing?"

"Why didn't you tell me you found out Callie had a boyfriend?" Mandy asked directly.

"I'm sorry?" Detective Ferguson almost seemed taken aback by her question.

"You found out she was seeing a guy, Fin Lentz. You knew about Steph Moore' blog and her posts about Hollywood."

"Ms. Knox, we wanted to follow every lead before we considered your daughter's case closed."

"Closed?" Mandy asked, surprised. "You haven't found her!"

"Ms. Knox, we did our best and followed every lead we could. Everything points to your daughter having run away and moved to Hollywood with her friend. We can't confirm the city she went to at this time, but we believe she's safe."

"How did she get there?"

"We don't know that—"

"She has no money! How we she planning on surviving out there? They have no car." Mandy could feel herself getting angry and tried to not say anything too bad to the detective. "I mean, she didn't leave me a note or give a call! This is not right! You need to confirm where she is."

"Listen," the detective said calmly, "I understand your concern here, but we can't locate her in a large city without any new info. I can give you the name of a few good private investigators I know. Maybe they can help locate her."

"Did you talk to my ex, Steve? He got back in town last night."

"No, but is sounds like you have," the detective said curtly. "And did he have any new information on the whereabouts of your daughter?"

"No," Mandy said quickly.

Mandy could hear the sound of something buzzing on the other end of the phone. "I'm sorry, Ms. Knox, but without more information, there isn't anything I can do to assist. I have to—"

"Where is Detective Lane? I want to talk to her!" Mandy demanded.

"She's not available right now. I can give you the number for the Los Angeles Police Department. You can file a missing persons case for your daughter with them, as she is likely in that city. I can give you the number for those private investigators as well if you like."

"Thanks for nothing!" Mandy slammed the phone receiver down, ending the call.

CHAPTER EIGHTEEN

Detective Alda Lane

Alda stood on top of a slightly sloping hill, overlooking the body of a young woman. Though it was a sunny day without a cloud in the sky, the thick trees around it shaded her from sun exposure. A shallow babbling brook splashed up against her body, with water flowing underneath her having a reddish hue. Her once yellow dress was dirtied from exposure from the outside and wherever else she had been before being left in the woods.

I should have done more, Alda thought.

Detective Ferguson showed his credentials to a uniformed officer outside of the police tape. He nodded his head as he went under the yellow tape.

"Sorry, Lane," he said. "Got held up at the office. What do we have?"

Alda nodded towards the body of the young woman. "Looks like you got your murder case after all, Ferg."

Ferguson looked down into the tree line at the body of a young woman. Her yellow dress flapped from side to side with the breeze. Her matted brunette hair was dirtied from the mud around her.

Ferguson lowered his sunglasses to take a better look. "That's not who I think it is, is it?"

"Callie Knox," she answered. "Forensics say her body was placed here within the last few hours. We're going to need her mother to identify the body. Her face is badly battered, so it's hard to tell."

Alda walked towards the girl's body. "Feels like the Hardwauld sisters all over. They were found in the woods like this. Brutally murdered."

"I just talked to Amanda Knox," Ferg said, amazed. "I told her we closed the missing persons case on her daughter. Fuck. This is bad."

"I asked you to hold off on having that talk with Knox," Alda said, mildly annoyed. "This is going to make it so much worse now."

"Amanda Knox did tell me something interesting at least. Steve Knox is back in town. Coincidentally, he came last night."

"That is interesting," Alda admitted. "I'm organizing a search today around these woods."

"I take it you believe Steph Moore is around here somewhere?"

Alda nodded her head. "Like I said, I'm getting the Hardwauld sister vibes again. They were found close together. Let's get a patrol car to sit outside Steve Knox's house until we get there. We should go see Amanda Knox first. Ask her to go to the corner's office. Forensics is done here."

"You honestly think Steve Knox could do this to his own daughter? You said the other victims were sexually abused." Ferguson wiped his forehead. "That's hard to believe. Left out here in the middle of the woods, where hikers visit. He's asking her to be found."

"That's right," Alda admitted. "A trail is not too far from here. Some off the trail hiker found her." Alda kneeled down beside what used to be the face of Callie Knox. The limp arms of her body were stretched out to Alda as if pleading for her help. "She wasn't raped though. Forensics did a quick check onsite. No semen, nothing. She was found dead, fully clothed. All the other bodies were found naked, sexually abused." She pointed at the body. "Her panties are on, and the coroner said there was no sign of sexual penetration. He's going to do a full review though to confirm."

"Maybe it's not your guy," Ferg said.

Alda shook her head. "The battered face, that was part of his MO." She took out a pen from her long jacket pockets. "This is another reason." She lifted the dirty dress up, revealing the body's midsection. Sliced into her was the word 'slut.' "He marked her, just like the others. This one is marked with a more aggressive word though. Usually, it's more…nice. 'Angel' or 'precious.' 'Slut' is something else. Not like him."

"If Steph Moore isn't already dead," Ferg said, "she will be soon." Alda nodded in agreement.

Alda looked at the young woman's face, using her pen to brush her dark, dirtied hair from her lips. She noticed a blotch of dark mud in the corner of her lip.

I will get him this time, she thought.

"I tell you what, Lane," Ferg said. "You go to Steve's house with the uniforms. I'll go speak to Ms. Knox in person. Have her come down to the coroner. It's on me to tell her what happened here. I'll finalize some details about the search party before leaving."

Alda stood up. "Sounds good, Ferg." She took one last look at the body before leaving the scene.

CHAPTER NINETEEN

Mandy

Mandy sat outside her front porch, sipping tea. It was hard to believe the last few days had actually happened. It felt like a nightmare roller coaster. She needed to calm herself after talking to Detective Ferguson over the phone.

What else is there for me to do now? The case was closed.

She took another sip of her tea, wishing it was anything but tea. She shouldn't have taken that shot from Fin, but she had. How easily a whole year of sobriety vanished.

After all she had been through though, she knew if she had only one drink through the past few days, that she had done pretty well. She would have handled this much worse a few years ago.

Mandy looked out at the blue sky. There was barely a cloud. It was a nice day, but she planned to do nothing with it. Mandy thought about calling James, but with her husband in town, she knew she couldn't risk it.

Steve was on his own mission now. He said he was going to somehow fix the mess that Mandy had made. She worried what that meant but tried to let those thoughts go.

There's nothing I can do. There's nothing Steve can do. She's gone, for a better life. Someday, she will come back home. Pat Moore was right—there was nothing she could do about it.

Mandy thought about moving to L.A. What was holding her here in Cranston? There were plenty of waitressing jobs in Hollywood. She might even get lucky some day and spot her daughter. Maybe she would be her server. The other waitresses would shriek when they spotted a celebrity like Callie Knox walking into their restaurant, and then Mandy would get to surprise them by telling them that was her daughter. They would embarrass her right there, in front of everyone in the restaurant, while the brunch crowd clapped.

A police cruiser drove up to her driveway. Detective Ferguson got out of the vehicle and waved at her.

"Not you again," Mandy said. "I thought my case was *closed*."

Detective Ferguson had a somber face, biting his lower lip, as he approached her porch. "Ms. Knox, I'm sorry for how that phone call went, I really am. I have some bad news."

"What the hell are you talking about?" Mandy demanded, standing up from her chair.

"We found a body of a young woman today, in the woods. She was wearing a yellow sundress."

Mandy burst into tears. Her legs buckled suddenly, and she landed hard on the porch. Detective Ferguson attempted to pick her up, but she shrugged his hand off. "You told me she ran away! You said that! Case! Closed!"

"I need your help to identify her at the coroner's office," Fegruson said. "We need your help. We need to catch whoever did this to her."

"You have her picture," Mandy said between sobs. "Just use it to identify her. I can't see her like that."

"It's not that easy," Ferguson said. "We need your help."

"Why wouldn't it be easy? Look at her face," she said. Ferguson lowered his head. "Oh my god! What did that monster do to her face?"

"Think of Steph Moore, Mandy," Ferguson said. "We need to find her. We need to catch whoever did this."

Mandy stood up from the floor, wiping a tear. "Fine."

"You can get in the cruiser if you want," he said.

Mandy shook her head. "No, give me some time to collect myself."

"I can wait in the cruiser for—"

"I'd like you to leave, please," Mandy said.

Ferguson nodded his head. "I'm sorry, Ms. Knox, I really am. I can promise you we will find out what happened and who did this." Ferguson took out a card and a pen, jotting something on the back of it. "Here's the address of coroner's office. Please come as soon as you can."

Mandy took the card and went inside her home, shutting the front door behind her. She immediately picked up the phone, dialing his number, but he didn't pick up.

"James," Mandy pleaded into the phone. "Just come over when you get this."

She hung up the phone, trying her best to control her emotions. She wanted to cry, but instead, her body shook. She could feel herself loosing balance. She took several deep breaths. She looked at the card Ferguson gave her. She knew where the office was.

She took her time, getting into her car. She continued to breathe deeply until she parked beside the building. Mandy pushed opened the doors and walked inside. The woman at the counter greeted her, but she ignored her.

When she got what she came for, she brought them to the front counter.

"Someone's having a party," the woman behind the counter said with a smile.

"Something like that," Mandy managed to say.

The cashier bagged the bottle of whiskey and pushed the case of beer towards Mandy. "Have a great day."

She loaded her liquor into the trunk, opening the case of beer and taking a few cans with her to the front seat. Once inside the driver's seat, she opened one immediately and let the cool taste of beer slip down her throat.

An hour later, she had downed six cans and one glass of whiskey with cola. Music was blasting from her radio speakers. Mandy finished the last bit of a can and threw it across the room, almost tripping on her couch. She steadied herself.

For a moment, she thought of Callie. She ran to the fridge, opening up another beer, gulping it.

This is not my fault, Mandy thought. *How dare he say that to me!*

She picked up the phone and dialed his number. Steve didn't pick up.

"Steve! Are you home?!" Mandy yelled. "Pick up the phone, you *piece of shit*. Callie is dead! She's dead, and it's not my fault. It's yours. You were never there! Maybe if you acted like a father for once in your life, she would still be here! By the way, I hope you are listening to this, I'm fucking your brother! I love James! I think I always have! The only thing I hate about him is he's your brother."

A knock at the front door startled her. She hung up the phone.

Steve is here already?

Mandy ran to her bedroom as fast as she could manage. She rummaged through her closet until she found her handgun. She clicked the safety off and went back to the front door. She peeked through the peephole and saw James.

Mandy opened the door and smiled at him. James saw the gun and raised his hands up. "What are you doing? Jesus, you're a mess."

Mandy dropped the gun to her side. "She's dead."

The day Callie left.

How do you say goodbye?
One moment, you're here, the next, gone.
What will she think, my mother?
Will she hate me forever? One day, I hope to meet with her again, I do. Once I'm settled in and have figured out my own life.
Maybe someday, I'll have a kid myself. I rarely think of having a child. They ruin your body, and that makes it hard to keep up with Hollywood's standards.
If I do have a kid someday, maybe Mom and I can take her to Disneyland.
I decided to call Mom on the way, maybe once we hit the state of California. I'll find a payphone. Steph laughed when I asked her if she'd tell her mom.
How do you say goodbye though? It was much easier to say nothing and leave…
Does that make me a coward?
Leaving Cranston soon, and all I can think about is her.
I hope she knows that I love her, I just don't need her right now…
I need to live for me.

CHAPTER TEWNTY

Detective Alda Lane

Alda felt defeated when she returned to the station to meet up with Ferg.

The system was meant to shield pieces of shit like Steve Knox, she knew, but she would bring him down one way or another.

Alda had him tagged as the killer of Theresa and Karen Hardwauld and those other girls. His mother owned a large property in the county. He could have brought his victims there without much interruption. They'd brought him in for questioning back then, and he'd lawyered up. He wouldn't say a word. She didn't meet Mandy though, or Callie. She'd known of his young teenaged daughter and wife at the time.

If only Ferg knew how much she did to find out if it was Steve. The county was filled with trails. It was very easy to accidently find yourself on someone's property without knowing. She'd scoured the large property of the Knox acreage, but found nothing. Alda was looking to really put the heat on Steve, when evidence of Ryland appeared on his truck.

When Alda saw Steve Knox again today, she knew better than to expect him to pour out his guilt when she knocked on his door with the other uniformed cops but didn't expect his response.

"Get the fuck off my property," he said. "Stop harassing me.

If I see you sneaking around, I'll assume your trespassing and deal with you how I would any man who dares to do that." He looked down at a sign on his front door that read "Trespassers Will be Shot."

It only cemented in her mind that she was onto something.

Ferg greeted her when she walked past his desk. "Big update for you." He stopped and looked at Alda. "Where's Steve Knox?"

"He wouldn't come to the station. I don't have enough to arrest. He basically said he would be ready with a lawyer if he sees me again." Alda plopped herself into her desk. "Not even when I told him that we found a body that matches his daughter description, would he say much. He refused to help. Can't believe it. Did Ms. Knox already go to the coroner's office with you?"

"She didn't show up. I tried calling her, but she didn't pick up."

"Why didn't you go back and get her?" Alda asked with a sigh.

"New development," he said, placing a file in her hands.

CHAPTER TWENTY-ONE

Mandy

Mandy sat in front of the television, watching a VHS of her daughter in the school play. She sipped coffee and water as she wiped her tears. James sat on the couch behind her with a glass of water.

On the television, Callie was playing the Virgin Mary. Mandy smiled at the screen every time her daughter spoke.

"That's my daughter," she said to James without looking behind her. "Can you believe it? That was her."

She had taped the play. On stage was a manger, with real goats, horses, and chickens. The audience laughed when one of the large horses defecated on stage.

At one point, the camera turns to Mr. Peterson. He pointed at Callie on stage and gave the camera a thumbs-up.

Beside him was Mr. Greyson, speaking to a young female student. If it weren't Mandy's television, she would have thrown her coffee at the screen in anger. When she'd spoken with Detective Ferguson, she hadn't mentioned what she'd found out about him. It might've just been a rumor, but it definitely needed to be looked into more.

She wondered if he'd ever pressured her daughter. Callie did say she had to study for his test. Even though she hadn't even taken the test, maybe there was some truth to that.

A knock at the door made her spill some coffee on the floor. She used the bottom of her shirt to wipe it up. James answered the door. "Oh, hey," he said. "I'm trying to sober her up a bit. She took the news as well as you think she would." He turned to Mandy, who lay in front of the television. "It's Detectives Lane and Ferguson."

"Tell them to go away!" she barked back. "I can't take this anymore."

"Can I come inside, Mr. Knox?" Detective Lane asked James. James stepped aside for the detectives to come in. "Patricia Moore has identified the body of her daughter, Steph." Mandy looked up at her. "It wasn't Callie, Ms. Knox."

She looked at Ferguson. "But you said it was Callie. She was wearing the yellow sundress, right?"

"Steph Moore was wearing your daughter's clothes," Alda said. "We're not sure why though."

"I'm sorry again, Ms. Knox," Fegruson said. "We were hoping to identify the body with you, but the coroner's office called me soon after I left your home, telling me they'd made a mistake."

"How do they know it's not Callie?"

Alda pointed at her nose. "They found a hole for a nose piercing on the body. You reported to us that Callie had no piercings besides her ears. Patricia Moore has already identified her."

"What does this mean now?" James asked.

Ferguson spoke up. "It's a homicide case now, and both Detective Lane and I will continue to work it. We wanted to come here and give you the news about your daughter, Ms. Knox."

"Your daughter is still considered missing but with foul play involved," Lane said.

"Is my daughter dead already?" Mandy asked.

The detectives exchanged a look. "We don't know yet, Mandy," Lane said. "We're organizing a search of where we found Steph. We have quite a bit of people who have signed up."

"I need to be there," Mandy said.

"I'll be there too," James said, standing beside her.

"That's good," Ferguson said. "Mr. Knox, I'd like to talk to you at our office tonight as well. We want to rule out everyone we can before we follow more leads."

James looked at Mandy. "I was helping her sober up a bit. Can I come by in a few hours?"

Mandy held his hand. "I'm fine, really. Just go with them." Mandy looked at Detective Lane. "How was Steph killed? Detective Ferguson said she couldn't be identified with a picture."

Detective Lane raised her hand. "I'm sorry, Mandy, I can't say. It's an active investigation now."

Mandy tried to focus, the booze in her system making it difficult, but she still could put things together. "So Steph's body was found in the woods? Her face beaten. Was she raped? Naked?

The officers exchanged a look. "Why are you asking, Mandy?" Detective Lane asked.

Mandy lowered her head. "I know you were involved in the Hardwauld murders. They were found, along with those other girls, naked and abused, their bodies discarded in the woods like a dead animal." James looked at Mandy with a stern look, but she didn't care. She pictured Callie lying on the ground, surrounded by trees. "Don't tell me this isn't related. I may not be sober, but I can put two and two together!"

Detective Lane cleared her throat. "I can't say anything about an act—"

"Active investigation, I know," Mandy said in a nasty tone. "Will you be there tomorrow as well?"

"Of course," Detective Lane said. "Get some good rest, Ms. Knox. Don't feel pressure to come tomorrow though. This is tough on anyone. It's okay if you're not there. Right now, you need to take care of yourself."

"What you really mean is, stop drinking, Mandy," she said with a bitter laugh.

"Callie needs you to help us right now," Detective Alda said.

"I need you to find my daughter."

CHAPTER TWENTY-TWO

It was already midway through the search, and nothing had been found in the woods where Steph Moore' body was found. Mandy stopped and leaned against a tree, taking a sip of water. The whole day, Mandy had walked with the rest of the volunteers in rows, searching the area. They would start in one area, and then move to a different spot, making sure to double-check each area with a new set of eyes.

Detective Lane directed them mostly.

She was surprised to see the number of people that had showed up. She spotted Principal Blacksmith and Mr. Peterson. There were some young students with them. Mr. Peterson had told her they were from the drama club and wanted to help.

Mandy had thanked them all for coming.

Mandy finished another sip of water. James walked up beside her. "You okay?" Mandy nodded her head. "Good," James said. "Last night was bad, Mandy. I've never seen you like that, not since before you got better. Promise me you'll keep it under control."

"I will," Mandy lied.

Detective Lane walked up beside them. "Hey," she said. "I wanted to check in with you both before leaving. Detective Ferguson will lead the search now."

Mandy reached a hand out to her. "Hey, I'm sorry about last night. This has been a lot."

"I understand, Mandy, I do." She reached out and shook

Mandy's hand. "I won't stop until we find her."

"Is my ex-husband showing up today?" Mandy asked. She looked at James briefly, then back at the detective.

"I don't believe so," she said.

Mandy sighed. "Even now, he's useless."

Detective Lane gave a thin smile. "I'm sure you had plenty reasons why you didn't want him in your life anymore. I may want to ask you more questions about your husband soon. Would that be okay? Could you come by the station again?"

Mandy nodded her head.

"Why?" James asked. "Is he a suspect?"

Detective Lane didn't respond. "I'll check in with Deceive Ferguson soon as well. It's hot outside, so make sure you take plenty of breaks."

"Did you hear about Mr. Greyson and Steph?" Mandy asked the detective. "Rumor was that they were romantically involved. You read her blog, right?"

"We did," she said. "We're still following leads. I did hear this from some students already. A few different teachers names came up though. I'll catch up with you soon, Mandy."

As Detective Lane walked to her car, Mandy swore under her breath. "She's not going to find my daughter, is she? Look what she has us doing all day."

James looked at Mandy with a raised eyebrow. "Are you okay? Mandy, have you been drinking?"

"Smell my breath if you don't believe me," she said. "The police work so slowly. Whoever killed Steph and those other girls has Callie. I know it. That article we read about the murders, it said the sisters were found together. Together!" Mandy took another sip of her water. "If Callie were dead, she would be here. The killer murdered Steph, but not Callie. Why? We know Steph is the rebel. You only need to read a few of her blogs to find that out. The killer keeps the girls, sometimes for weeks. Maybe he decided to get rid of Steph."

James grabbed the bottle of water from Mand, taking a sip. "Vodka? Come on, Mandy!"

"He has my daughter! And what is anybody doing about it? We've been searching in these woods for hours! I'm going to talk to Mr. Greyson myself. It takes the police decades to go talk to the suspects around this town! I can do it, right now! Come with me."

James stood still. "Mandy, get help, please."

"I am the only one helping here!" Mandy barked.

CHAPTER TWENTY-THREE

Detective Alda Lane

Alda sat in her sports car parked on the highway. Ferg walked up to the driver's window, knocking. Alda rolled down the window.

"Where you off to?" he asked.

"Wanted to follow up on something," she said curtly. Ferguson lowered his sunglasses, peering at her. "Ryland Moore. I called the prison. I need to see him. I know he's not the killer, and he needs to know I'm going to get him out. I need to tell him. It won't take long. I'll follow up with that teacher, Mr. Greyson, right after."

"Did you forget you have a partner, Alda?" Ferg asked, unamused. "You're not supposed to go alone all the time. You know how this works."

Alda pointed at her watch. "Time's ticking. You said that to me, right? We don't have much time until we find Callie Knox somewhere next. We need to cover as much ground as we can. Keep up with the search party and with the uniforms searching the nearby farms. The coroner's office found hay in her Steph Moore' bra, as well as a trace of some animal defecation. We know the killer keeps them somewhere for days, or months sometimes, then dumps them when he's done with them."

"Alda, get out of the car and talk to me," Ferg said.

Alda shook her head. "I'm not finding the real Callie in the forest like Steph. We need to move on this, Ferg."

"The other detectives in major crimes are all dropping their cases for a day to help with the search."

"I know that, and good," Alda said.

"Who's the rookie now?" Ferg asked. "You can't take this personal, Lane. If this shit is getting to you, talk to one of the shrinks on staff. I won't tell anyone if you do."

Alda laughed. "Take your Kleenex box and shove it, Ferg. There's a lot of farms out here, and not a lot of time."

Alda turned the ignition, rolled the window up, and took off down the highway. It was only thirty minutes to Essex County Prison. Along the way, she thought of the brutal crime scenes of Steph Moore and the Hardwauld sisters. Their pretty faces bashed in. Theresa Hardwauld had had the word 'beauty' marked on her chest, while her little sister had the word 'pretty.' Karen's body was much smaller than her sister's, so the killer had had to invert his knife to carve the words so that they were large enough to read.

She would not let the same happen to Callie Knox, if she was even still alive.

Alda made arrangements for the prison staff to have Ryland Moore in an interview room waiting for her when she arrived. She wasn't disappointed when she saw Ryland patiently waiting in the room. Guards stood outside, with a man wearing a suit stepping toward her.

"Detective Lane," he said. "Thank you for calling ahead. We made all arrangements for you to talk with Mr. Moore. The cameras are not recording as you have requested."

From inside the room, Ryland raised both hands, chained with handcuffs, waving his fingers.

Alda shook his hand. "Thank you—"

"I'm the warden. Warden Michaels. Let me know if you need anything else."

"How is he doing?" Alda asked.

"We gave him the news about his daughter right away. He took it as any man would who found out their daughter was murdered."

Alda nodded her head and walked into the room.

"Detective Alda Lane," Ryland said with a sly smile. "The worst day of my life, and I get to see you again. How sweet."

"I'm sorry to hear about Steph," she said in a low tone.

"Being a cop, you probably had plenty of run-ins with her, eh?" he said with a smile. "She was always the type to get into trouble. Pat tells me she's been into drugs, sex with strangers, and all sorts of things." He lowered his head. "Look where that got her." He raised his head with a fake smile. "At least this time, you know for sure it wasn't me who did it, right?"

Alda breathed in deeply. "I told you the day I put the cuffs on you that I didn't think you killed those girls."

Ryland banged the table hard. The guards outside peered through the glass. Alda put a hand up towards them to let them know she was fine.

"It was my job, Ryland. The DA told me to. They felt they had enough evidence to convict, despite me telling them not to charge."

"What evidence again?" Ryland said, putting his chained hands to his ear. "Right. I'm a truck driver. I've been to the places where some of those girls were killed and kidnapped. I have a storm cellar, where you thought I held those girls' captive, even though Pat and Steph and I lived not far away. But did they find any evidence of anybody being held down in the cellar? No! Just that goddamn hairclip from some young hooker I had on the road. That was it!"

"I know your story, Ryland. You told me this before. I couldn't do anything about it."

Ryland raised his hands. "Of course not. Instead, I rotted in prison for the last five years, while my child had to be raised without her father! I could have prevented her from going down this path! I could have done something to help her! You killed her! You killed my daughter, Detective!"

Alda breathed in deep. "I believe everything you're saying. I need you to hear this from me, I'm going to help you."

"How?" Ryland said laughing. "Let me know before I rot a full life sentence?"

"I think your daughter was killed by him." Ryland dropped his hands on the table. "I'm going to find him. The killer is still out there. I know that for sure now."

"Then what the fuck are you here talking to me for?" Ryland mused. It was a good question, Alda knew. Why did she feel the urge to see him today? Inside, she'd felt she had to. She knew she'd made a mistake the day she read him his rights and charged him with murder, but now, she had proof.

"I'll see you soon, Ryland." Alda stood from the chair and left the room promptly.

"Don't wait another five goddamn years to see me, Detective!"

She had made several promises today, some she worried she couldn't keep.

Callie Knox could already be dead.

The day Callie went missing.

Today is the first day of the rest of my life. I'm writing this on the road! Fin agreed to drop us off at a bus stop in the city. In five days, we will be in Hollywood, California! I can't use any more exclamation marks!!!
It was hard leaving—

He ripped the pages of her journal in front of her.

"Callie, this is all garbage! All of it!" He paced across the room, ripping the rest of her journal.

Callie Knox sat in her prison-like cell, watching him, knowing better than to talk back. It had been a whole day since she saw Steph. From the look in his eyes, Callie knew she was gone forever.

"Your journal lacks passion. Its all so high school! I expected more from you. For one thing, I'm barely in this! This whole journal is garbage." He turned around, throwing her journal in a bin. "You and I both know he didn't drive you anywhere! He left you. And who saved you? Me!"

Callie sat quietly, cross-legged, making sure to listen attentively to what he said. He didn't like it if you didn't pay attention to him. He didn't like it if you weren't looking at him. He didn't like a lot of things.

He was starting to be meaner to her as well, after Steph. He used to change out the bucket she used as a toliet twice a day. Since he's taken Steph away, he hadn't changed it at all.

He waved a hand at Callie dismissively, then moved to the other side of the storm shelter, playing with a large hunting knife. He enjoyed tossing it into a wooden box on the floor, practicing his aim at times, but mostly, he enjoyed showing it to Callie.

"My father had a pig farm. You know about that, because I told you. When he died, my mother kept the farm going. She used this to kill his pigs." He raised the knife and mocked slicing his throat. "She took me with her when she did it. She said it was to *toughen me up*. 'You're too much of a good boy,' she would tell me.

She tried to get me to do it too, sometimes. I had a hard time at first. The first time I refused, she would hit me. Sometimes, she'd even hit me with the butt of this knife. Every time I refused, she would hit harder, until I slit the throat of that pig."

Callie wasn't sure what he wanted her to say. "I'm so sorry —"

"Shut up!" He put the knife down. "Stop being so perfect! Stop being a pussy." He smiled at her. "Stop being so *good*."

"What do you mean?" Callie asked, confused.

"That's the perfect word for you," he said with a wicked smile. "Do you want to know the word I gave to your little friend?"

Callie lowered her head. "No."

"*Slut!* It suited her well, I thought. You're different though, at least I hope so." He took a few steps up the short ladder, pushing open the trap door. "Don't move, I'll be right back."

Callie looked around the storm shelter. The cell was made out of steel, and the bars unmovable, likely cemented. She and Steph had tried for hours to free themselves when he wasn't around. She looked at her muddy feet. The shelter was mostly dirt, clay actually, and hard to remove with your hands. He'd laughed when he noticed Steph had managed to dig a few inches of earth out.

Steph was dead now, and she would be next. Callie couldn't take it anymore. The only way out seemed to be how Steph did it —fight. When she'd hit him hard in the groin, he'd immediately taken her out of her cell, dragging her out of the shelter, ripping Callie's dress she had on.

That was the last she saw of Steph.

Days ago, they were having the best time of their lives. It had been Steph's idea to change their outfits. Callie told her on the day they were leaving that she needed to be someone else that day to make it through. Steph had laughed and said she could change into her. She'd taken off her clothes off right there and demanded Callie give her the dress.

When Fin had picked them up at the school's bleachers,

he'd almost dropped his mouth wide open at Callie with her new look. He'd said it reminded him of Olivia Newton John at the end of *Grease*. She could tell he'd also been interested immediately in Steph's new look.

The deal had been simple—Steph would give Fin the rest of her weed, and he would drive the girls to the city. They hadn't even made it out of the school parking lot when Fin got fresh with Steph. Steph had slapped him in the face. He'd called them prude bitches and kicked them out.

That was when he had seen them.

He climbed back down into the storm caller, a book in his hand. "Here's another journal. Start over. I want to see some passion in your writing and more of me. I have to leave, but I'm never far away. I can't wait to see what you write this time." Callie began to cry, but it only made his smile wider. "Don't be a bad little girlie," he said. "You know what happens to bad little girlies, right? Keep being the *good* girl you are, and I'll keep you longer."

CHAPTER TWENTY-FOUR

Mandy

Mandy Knox knew she was intoxicated, but it didn't matter. Time was all that mattered. So what if she needed more courage to do what she had to do to find her daughter? Nobody else was doing anything. Police had procedures, ways to do things. Mandy could be more direct.

She parked in the Cranston High parking lot beside the football field. She tossed her purse over her shoulder and looked out at the bleachers, hoping she would spot Callie sitting there, waving for her.

She had arrived just in time for the end of the school day. Teenagers started to fill the parking lot and loaded themselves into vehicles. One young man clapped his hands slowly, and others joined him. Another girl tossed some notebooks in a trash-can outside the school doors.

Mandy walked inside, taking her time to remember where his classroom was. It didn't help that her whole world was spinning already. She leaned against some lockers. She could feel her vodka filled stomach twirl inside her. The heat from walking around all day in the woods didn't help. She lowered her head and covered her mouth, but it didn't help.

Her mouth erupted with vomit, splattering some lower lockers.

"What the fuck?!" a young girl shouted near her, followed by other students laughing.

"It's not funny," Mandy yelled, but the teenagers' laughs continued. She stood up. The laughter reminded her of the phone call with the woman's laugh from that night. "Callie!" she yelled into the crowd of teenagers.

"Are you okay?" a boy asked. He tried to help her by putting an arm around her.

"Don't fucking touch me!"

A screeching sound came over the sound system in the hallways. "This is Principal Blacksmith. Thank you, students, for another wonderful year! Enjoy your summer. See you next school year, and for our graduating students, we wish you all the best!"

Mandy laughed to herself. She took a few more steps and saw a flight of stairs. She remembered his classroom was somewhere on the second floor. She took her time with each stair until she managed to make it to the top. One student knocked into her, almost causing her to lose her balance. She held on to the stair rail at the top of the stairs.

The young woman who'd bumped into her apologized and stared at Mandy.

"It's okay," Mandy said, placing a hand on her shoulder. "Where is Mr. Greyson's classroom?"

"Down the hall," she said pointing. "Room 210." Mandy nodded her head and continued down the hallways. She could tell it was the last day of school by how fast the teenagers emptied their lockers and almost ran out of the building. The hallways were nearly empty by the time Mandy spotted room 210.

She peeked through the glass window of the door and spotted Mr. Greyson. "You piece of shit," she said quietly to herself. She reached into her purse to make sure that the gun was still there. She wrapped her hand around the grip of the gun, keeping her hand hidden in her purse.

Mandy heard Mr. Greyson raising his voice and pointing at something.

Someone else is in the room.

Mandy rolled her head to the other side of the window and spotted Detective Lane, raising her hands at him. Lane lowered her hand and brushed it against the side of her waist, revealing her gun.

Mandy lowered her head immediately. She wanted to press Mr. Greyson for more information but was not dumb enough to do it in front of Detective Lane.

Fuck.

Mandy felt energy exploding inside her. All she wanted was to go inside and start shooting. She contained herself and even managed to rationalize that Mr. Greyson might not be involved in this at all.

Detective Lane had beaten her here, but Mandy could follow more of her own leads. Mandy Knox snuck past the room, back through the hallway, and down the stairs. She almost kicked the front doors of the school open when she was startled by a woman's voice behind her.

"Ms. Knox!" Mandy looked behind her at Principal Blacksmith, who stared at her with her arms crossed. "What are you doing?"

"Whatever I need to do," Mandy answered, walking outside. She opened her car door and spotted Principal Blacksmith watching her leave. She had a radio in her hand and was speaking into it.

Mandy drove off down the street, parking on the side of the road after ten minutes of driving aimlessly. She picked up the almost empty water bottle. She drank the last bit of vodka and tossed the bottle into the backseat with a curse.

Digging her hand into her purse, she took out the handgun. She laughed to herself before putting it to her temple. She closed her eyes in anticipation, thinking the last thing she would hear was the click of the trigger.

Breathing in deep, she opened her eyes slowly and spotted a sign that said, 'Ace High Club. Two miles ahead on the left.' Mandy laughed again, putting the car back in drive, and took off down the road. She parked in the bar's parking lot, taking up two spots.

She took a few steps towards the bar when she noticed a girl laughing. There was something about the laugh that caught her attention. She followed the side of the building, hearing people talk nearby. She peered around the corner and saw Jessica Summers kissing Fin. Jessica laughed again, and this time, Mandy knew exactly where she had heard that voice. Fin pushed Jessica up against the side of the building, pulling her hair to the side and kissing her neck. Jessica covered her mouth, gasping.

Mandy smiled, reaching into her purse. "How about that drink, Fin?"

Fin and Jessica turned to her.

"What?" Fin asked.

"That drink," Mandy repeated. "Why don't the three of us get fucked up in the alley, right now? Just like you did with Callie and Steph!"

"She's drunk!" Jessica laughed. "She can barely stand."

"And you," pointed Mandy. "I know it was you who's been calling my house. Why?"

"Get her out of here, Fin," Jessica said. "She's scaring me."

"Listen, Cas' mom," Fin said, "just chill, okay. We—"

"It's Callie!" Mandy yelled back. She gripped the gun in her purse, took it out, and pointed it at him. "Now, where is she?"

Fin raised his hands. "I swear I don't know!" Jessica started to cry. "Look," Fin said lowering his hand, "I was supposed to drive Steph and Cas—I mean, Callie, to the bus stop in in the city. We fought though. I left them at the bleachers at school that night."

"Why didn't you say that before!" Mandy barked, raising the gun again.

"You really think I'm going to tell the cops I was the last person to see Steph Moore alive?"

Mandy looked at Jessica. "Why were you calling my house?"

Jessica raised her hands and closed her eyes, screaming. Mandy grabbed her hair, pointing the gun at her temple. "Shut up!" Mandy yelled, and Jessica listened. Fin got closer to them but backed off when Mandy pointed it towards him. "I know it was you calling me, but why?"

Fin raised his hands, begging. "Please, it wasn't her idea. It was mine. The pig's blood! Jessica always called her a skank pig, so I thought it would be funny. I know a butcher. He's a regular at the bar. We got the blood in a jar and threw it on your porch. We tried calling the house to laugh at her, but Callie hung up right away."

"Leave us alone!" shouted Jessica.

Mandy grabbed her hair tighter between her fingers and raised the gun up. Fin attempted to grab Mandy's arm, but she shrugged him off and whacked the side of his face with the handgun. Fin dropped to the ground, covering his bleeding face and screaming in pain.

"You're fucking crazy!" Jessica said, dropping to her knees and cradling Fin in her arms. Mandy looked down at Fin and Jessica in shock. A large gash on the side of Fin's face was gushing out blood. "Jesus! Look what you did to him!" she shouted at Mandy. "We don't know where she is! Leave us alone! Fuck you and leave us alone!"

"Hey, what's going on back there?!" a voice shouted. A tall man walked into the alley, looking at Fin.

Mandy brushed past the man's shoulder. "He needs a doctor." Mandy got into her car and took off down the road.

She didn't stop until she got to his home. Mandy parked her car in his long driveway and pounded on the door until she heard the door unlock.

James opened the door partly with a frightened look. "Oh god, you have blood on you," he said.

"I did something bad," Mandy said, crying. "Very bad." She held out her purse. "Take my purse, please. Before I do something worse."

"You shouldn't have come," he said quietly.

A larger hand wrapped around the door frame, opening the door fully. Steve stared at her with a wicked smile. "No, I'm glad she did."

CHAPTER TWENTY-FIVE

Detective Alda Lane

Alda drove to Cranston High, parking on the street. One student looked at her with a smile. "Nice ride," he said.

Alda nodded. She brushed her jacket to the side, showing him her badge. "I'm looking for Mr. Greyson's classroom."

"He was my science teacher," one of the other boys in the group said.

"Was?" Alda asked.

The boy shrugged. "Last day of school. I can take you to his room."

Alda followed the boy until they reached Carl Greyson's room. His door was open, and Alda peeked inside. The science teacher was talking to a few female students. Alda thanked the boy who brought her there and went inside.

"Mr. Greyson?" asked Alda, catching his attention immediately. "I was hoping we could chat." Alda looked at the young students until they realized they should leave.

Mr. Greyson looked at Alda with an arched eyebrow. "It's the last day of school. I'm trying to say goodbye to my students."

"This will only take a few moments, Mr. Greyson."

"Please, just call me Carl. It's summer, after all." He went around to his desk and sat down. "So, I'm guessing this is about Callie Knox or Steph."

Alda nodded. "Let's start with Steph. We're trying to get an idea of the people involved in her life, and your name continues to come up."

Carl looked around his empty room. He stood up promptly and walked toward the classroom door. Alda brushed the side of her jacket, placing her hand on her hip. She could access her gun quickly if needed.

Carl shut the door, muttering to himself, and turned to her. "I've honestly had enough of these accusations! How much more of this shit do I need to take?!"

"Sir, please lower your voice," Alda said calmly.

"No! Call my union! I don't want to do this shit over and over again!" He pointed at the detective. "Unless you're pressing charges, get the fuck out of my classroom!"

Alda rested her hand on the top of her duty belt, above her gun. "We can talk here or at the station," she said, raising her voice. She caught a glimpse of someone looking through the door of the window.

Students were always nosey. It was likely that boy who showed her to the room. Whenever cops showed up somewhere, everybody wanted to know what was happening, especially teenagers.

"Maybe we should just go to the station," Alda said calmly.

"No, that's okay," Mr. Greyson said more calmly. "I have dinner plans with my wife." A tear began to form in his eye. "Do you know what this school year was like for me? The staff thinks I'm fucking the students. The kids laugh at me in the hallway. I've already put in for a transfer! All because that girl wrote a stupid blog."

"So you didn't touch her?"

"No! I would never!" Carl put a hand on his head. "Do you know what these accusations have done to my marriage?"

Alda picked up the frame of the happy looking Mr. and Mrs. Greyson from his desk. His hand was resting across her shoulder as they booth smiled for the picture. "She is very beautiful," Alda said to him.

"Four months of couples therapy, and our marriage is still not where it was."

Alda looked at the picture again and noticed a student in costume behind them. They appeared to be in a barn. She looked at one of the students and noticed Callie's face. "Where was this picture taken?"

"Last semester," he answered. "Yes, that's Callie in the background. My wife and I went to the show."

Alda smiled when she noticed the large horse in the background. "Talk about quality props. Where is this?"

"They put on the play at an actual farm. I'm involved with production, so I go to most school plays." Carl put a hand on his forehead. "Right after that play, things took a real turn for me."

Alda placed the frame back on his desk. She noticed a side table filled with trophies. At the top of the plastic gold trophies was a person kicking.

"I really must be going now, Detective," he said. "Maybe we can meet up at your station. Tomorrow good for you? Around noon?"

"Are all of these yours?" Alda asked, looking at the multiple trophies and medals on the table. "Pretty impressive."

"I coach a girls' travel team," he said. "I coach the school's team too."

"Travel team," Alda repeated. "That must be tough on you right now."

"I took some time off from coaching this year," he said quietly. He lowered his head. "Principal Blacksmith was very understanding."

Alda looked at some of the other pictures around his desk. Another picture of him and his wife was taken outdoors in front of a large old home. The large white sided home had dark trimmed windows. It looked just like a farmhouse. "This your place?" The teacher nodded. "Looks beautiful. I was raised in a home that looked like this. I grew up in a small town." She smiled. "I used to hate it so much. Couldn't wait to get out of that town. A large backyard is nice to have, but what's the point if you're all by yourself in it?"

"It's definitely hard to maintain it too," he said with a laugh. "A pain really. The drive into the school is a lot too. This school is the closet to my home. When I transfer, I'll be having to travel even farther." He looked at his watch. "Well, I'm going to be—"

"You did teach Ms. Moore though, right? She was in your class this semester."

Mr. Greyson nodded his head. "That's right."

"What was her final grade?"

Mr. Greyson walked over to his desk. "I'll page Principal Blacksmith here. I think I need my union rep here too, if this is how you're going to treat me. I told—"

"She got a B. I looked into it," Alda said, cutting him off. "If that was for Callie, I would understand, but Steph, I heard she barely attended school. So what? She ditched school, getting mostly Ds in every class, according to her last report card, but somehow managed a B in yours?"

"That girl was—"

"A slut, right!?" Alda shouted. "That's what you thought of her. She was promiscuous. She wrote about it. I'm sure you read it too."

"No! I—"

"What did you do?"

"Nothing!" Mr. Greyson shouted. "She was the one who blackmailed me!"

CHAPTER TWENTY-SIX

Mandy

Steve slapped Mandy across the face and tossed her to the couch. "You fucking bitch!"

James shouted back, "Stop!" Steve threw a punch, but James dodged it. James pulled his hand back and struck Steve in the jaw.

It didn't phase his brother. "My wife!" he yelled at James. "How could you?"

"I told you I was in love with her when we were kids!" James shouted. "What did you do? You took her!"

"She didn't want a pussy like you," Steve shouted.

Mandy covered her face. She could barely see. She could already feel the welt below her eye where Steve had struck her. "Stop, Steve!" she yelled, but it was no good.

"I'm going to kill him!" he shouted as he attempted to tackle James. James stepped to the side but lost balance and fell. Steve crawled on top of his brother and landed a strike to his chest. James shouted out in pain.

The fire in James' large fireplace crackled beside them, and a hot ember shot out, burning out on the wooden floor.

Mandy looked inside her purse but struggled to find the gun. In her haste, the purse fell to the ground between couches. She leaned down to pick it up and stopped when she saw it.

A yellow hair scrunchie.

She looked up at Steve and James fighting on the floor. James reached out and grabbed a fire poker, hitting his brother across the side with it. Steve curled on the floor, screaming in pain. James stood over his brother, the poker raised in his hand.

"What is this?!" Mandy yelled, holding the scrunchie in her hand. James' mouth dropped. "This is Callie's! She was wearing it before she left that night. Why is it here? Why?!"

James lowered the poker. "I can explain everything!" he yelled.

"You told me you hadn't seen Callie in weeks! So why is this here?"

James raised his hands. "I swear, Mandy."

Mandy bent over, grabbing the purse, taking out the gun. She pointed it at James. "Where is she?!"

Steve kicked James' leg and brought him to the floor. Steve climbed on top of his brother's chest and hit him in the face several times. "My daughter! You piece of shit!" He struck him again, and James' body went limp for a moment. Steve placed his thick hands around his brother's neck and squeezed.

James' feet wiggled underneath his brother aimlessly. His arms reached out to Mandy as if pleading for her to help. His eyes bulged from their sockets, and his face flushed red.

Mandy looked down at the scrunchie, and back at James. She pointed the gun, closed her eyes, and squeezed the trigger.

CHAPTER TWENTY-SEVEN

Detective Alda Lane

Mr. Greyson cried. "People read that fucking blog of Steph's. Somehow, students thought it was me, I don't know why. Steph stayed after class, and she told me she would tell everyone that it was me unless I gave her a good grade. I didn't give her an A! Everybody would think it was me if I did! I gave a B."

Alda slipped her hand under her jacket, taking the safety off her gun, and turned to him. "So you killed the *slut*?"

"No! I didn't! I told my union everything. They were supposed to have my back. My rep and I approached Principal Blacksmith, and I told her what happened. She believes me. Let's call her here! She's probably still in her office."

` Alda continued to press him. "Where is Callie Knox? This is your moment to make things better."

"I don't know," he sobbed. Alda was beginning to believe him. Would the killer be this pathetic? She could picture the Hardwauld sisters. Their abdomens sliced with words.

Alda grabbed the picture of Mr. Greyson and his wife. She shoved it in his face and pointed at Callie. "Isn't she pretty? Beautiful, an angel? Pick your word." She pointed at the barn in the picture. "Is this where you're keeping her?"

He lowered his head. "No! Goddammit. That's not even my property. It's Mr. Peterson's. I just wanted to help with his plays!"

He covered his face with his fingers. "I just wanted to help. He always helps me with soccer. I didn't do anything wrong! I just wanted to be a part of my school! Help those girls!"

Alda took her hand off the trigger and looked at the trophy table. She picked up a large trophy from the girls' travel soccer team, examining it. At the bottom it said, 'Coach Carl Greyson and Assistant Coach Randall Peterson.'

She lowered the picture frame in her hand and shoved it in his face again. "Where is this farm?"

CHAPTER TWENTY-EIGHT

Callie

He paced the storm shelter, the journal clenched between his fingers, and smiled. "This is much better," he said to her. "'Dear Journal,' —a bit of a cliché way to start— 'the moment I saw Mr. Peterson, I knew I was in love. He's so young and handsome. Ever since I was in tenth grade and started drama with him, I've had a crush on him. Many of the girls felt the same, but I knew he liked me. He treats me like a *princess*.'" He looked at Callie a moment. "My mom used to say to me all the time—treat a girl like a princess, no matter what. She would have liked you." He looked away. "She's dead now. Not by me, I'd never do something like that. I was a *good* boy. Her *good son. Good.* I still like that word." Peterson looked down at the journal again, wiping a tear from his eye. "'Mr. Peterson chose me for the lead role in his play, because he loves me and I love him. I knew he would always be there for me and would never *hurt me.*'"

The drama teacher raised an eyebrow. "I like the sympathy you're trying to drag out of me. I'd *never* hurt you, Callie?"

Callie could feel the dampness of her earth cell, and it gave her a chill. He smiled at her again. She knew he wanted her to say something but didn't know how to respond.

"I just want your love," Callie answered. The more love she could show him, the longer she could live. The moment it faded, she knew she was dead. Steph had never played along. She'd laughed at how impotent he became around her.

"Well, love hurts sometimes, Callie," he said. "Didn't you ever learn that?" He took out his large knife from his leather sheaf on his hip. "*Naïve.* Maybe that should be your word. Now, take off your panties."

Callie lowered her head. She wanted to stay alive, but how much more could she take from him? Steph had known the kind of monster he was. How long would she be trapped down here with him? How much more could she really take before taking the same trip Steph did?

"Finish reading the journal, please?" Callie asked him. "I want you to read the whole thing. I spent a lot of time writing it."

He pointed a finger down. "Don't make me rip them off."

Callie screamed. Peterson took his knife and sliced it across the cell bars. "What did I tell you, Callie? No screaming! You don't want us to fight."

Callie calmed herself and took a deep breath. "I'm not *naïve,*" Callie said. "I knew what you wanted when you picked Steph and I up at school that night."

He laughed. "Did you?"

"I wanted to get to know you, but not like this!" Callie heard herself shout at the monster but would not let him near her again. "I'm a lady, *Randall.* A *princess.* Treat me with respect! What would your mother think?"

"Shut up, you—"

"With respect, Randall!" Callie shouted again. "Do not talk to me in that way."

Peterson threw the journal into Callie's cell. "Stop talking! I know what you're doing!" He took his knife and sliced into the cell, cutting Callie's hand. She screamed. "Look what you made me do! *Naïve!* You think I'm *naïve?*"

The trap door sprung open, and a woman dropped inside the shelter. She took a moment to stand but pointed a gun at Mr. Peterson.

"Police! Don't move!" she yelled.

"Detective Lane!" he shouted back. "What a *fucking* surprise! What are you even doing on my property?"

"Lower your weapon!" the detective woman shouted.

Mr. Peterson shrugged his shoulder and lowered his knife, but as he did, he whipped his arm down, tossing the knife into the detective's leg. She shot her weapon and missed him, shooting another bullet into the earthen ceiling. He charged the woman, jumping on top of her, holding her wrist that held her gun.

Callie stood up in her cell, trying to find a way to get out to help. Helpless, she watched as the monster wrapped his other hand around the woman's neck.

Callie grabbed the journal and threw it at him. "I fucking hate you!" she shouted. "Hate you. All of the students think you're a joke. A *pussy*! Just wait till I tell them how impotent you are! Peterson *can't get it up*! I'm going to tell them all!" Callie waited for him.

Maintaining his grip on the woman's neck, he turned to look at Callie. "You're next! You—"

Callie threw her bucket of urine and feces at him. He let go of the detective immediately, wiping his face. "You slut! You pig!"

Callie watched the detective slide out a handgun from her ankle holster, press it against the monster's chest, and pull the trigger several times. Mr. Peterson dropped to the floor, his body limp.

The officer covered her neck with her hands, coughing. She looked down at her leg and the knife that was still in it. She looked around the room and spotted a rope on the floor. She wrapped it several times above her wound and tied it.

"The keys!" Callie shouted. "They're in his pocket!"

Alda attempted to stand but struggled, falling back to the floor. She crawled over to Mr. Peterson's body. When she did, Callie noticed his foot moved slightly.

Callie screamed, but the detective aimed her weapon and fired it at his head. Red matter gushed from the other side of his temple, and his body was limp again.

"Alda!" a deep voice called from outside the storm shelter.

"Ferg?" she yelled back. "I'm hurt! I found her, she's alive." The detective smiled at Callie. "Callie Knox, we found you."

A tall man jumped into the storm shelter, a gun in his hand. "Are you okay?" he asked the female detective.

"The bastard got my leg good."

"I told you not to go in alone!" the tall officer said.

"At least I radioed for you," she said with a smile. "The keys are in his pocket." She pointed at Mr. Peterson's body. "Get Callie out of there." The female cop smiled at Callie. "I know someone who will be really happy to see you."

She didn't need to tell Callie who it was. She already knew.

CHAPTER TWENTY-NINE

Callie

Callie sat in an interview room. The officers had left the door open. She knew why and appreciated it.

How many days had she been down in that storm shelter with that monster?

She tried not to think about it. She was above ground again and felt safe.

She fixed her oversized police sweatshirt. She had barely eaten the last few days and felt like she was swimming in the small sized sweatshirt and jogging pants they'd given her.

Detective Ferguson walked into the room, a different woman at his side.

"Hi," the woman said. "My name is Theresa Shandro. I'm a social worker that works with the state police. I know the police have many questions for you, but it's okay if you want to wait."

"It's not a problem at all if you do want to wait," Detective Ferguson said.

Callie nodded her head. "That woman, the other detective, is she okay?

"Detective Lane is fine," Ferguson said. "She wanted to come here tonight, but the doctor wouldn't release her from his care. She needs emergency surgery, but she will be okay."

Callie nodded her head. "Thanks for letting me shower

here, and for the change of clothes, but when can I go home?"

The social worker looked at Ferguson.

"We're still trying to reach your mother and father," Ferguson answered. "I have some officers waiting at each of their homes."

"What about my uncle's house?" Callie asked. "My mom, she's been seeing him. They are together, I think."

Ferguson nodded his head. "Yes, we went by there too. We have left messages with everyone as well and paged your father. As soon as we can, I'll bring you home myself."

"I'd like to come too, just for a little bit, if that's okay, Callie," Theresa said, and Callie nodded.

"My mom, she keeps a key in the backyard. It's in one of those fake rocks," Callie said with a smile. "It's funny. I tell her how useless that fake rock is. The rest of the rocks are dark, and it's light. It's so obvious that it doesn't belong. Robbers could tell instantly what it's for. I guess we could just go whenever. We don't have to wait for my mom to be there." Callie worried about her. The day she left, her mother had been on the couch, with new drama brewing. With Callie gone, it wouldn't have taken much for her to go over the edge again. "Is my mom doing okay?"

Ferguson stiffened his lower lip. "No, she's been having a hard time with everything. I was hoping to let her know right away that we'd found you alive, but we can't find her."

Callie lowered her head. "Try the Ace High Club, it's a local bar. It was one of the places she used to go to often." She thought of Fin a moment and could feel anger. Her body stiffened. If Fin had just brought them to the bus station like he'd promised, none of this would have happened. Callie looked up at Detective Ferguson. "I'm okay. We can just talk here, but can we go back to my home after we're done?"

"Of course," Ferguson said, raising his hand. "So, what happened that first night?"

Mandy sighed. "I'm *naïve*." She smiled to herself. "That's the word for me, I guess. I met this talent agent a few months ago. He said I had promise. I mentioned to him that I wanted to go to college and leave for Hollywood after, or maybe New York. Somewhere where people were making a living with acting. He told me I was wasting my time and my youth. I decided in my mind to leave a little after. Steph, she was game, of course." Callie smiled and could feel a tear forming in her eye. She wiped it quickly. She'd loved having a friend who supported her like Steph. She remembered the time she'd spoken to Principal Blacksmith, pretending to be her mom.

"Why then? Why leave that day?" Ferguson asked. "It sounded like you were close to finishing school. What made you want to leave?"

Callie nodded her head. "I was out with Steph one night. We sort of went out sometimes, with Fin. He would sneak us booze from the bar he worked at. Anyway, Steph and I were walking around the town one night, when I spotted my uncle's car at a motel. He was teaching me to drive a few months ago. Anyway, I spotted my mom driving into the parking lot of the motel too. She went straight to a room, knocked on the door, and went inside." Callie could remember the anger she'd felt that night, that it couldn't be what she thought it was. There must have been a reason why the two of them were in a motel, besides the obvious. "I made Steph wait with me. It began to rain, but I wouldn't move until I saw them leave together. We hid under a roofed part of some office building. A few hours go by, and my uncle leaves the room. He gets into his expensive car and leaves. Another few minutes go by, and my mom comes out of the same room, fixing her hair into a ponytail, and leaves. I got home that night and asked her what she did. She told me she picked up a late shift at the diner." She laughed to herself. "I even said, you don't smell like coffee for a change. Mom told me that there were barely any customers and she was surprised Dean, the owner, let her finish her shift." Callie looked at Ferguson for a moment, then looked away. "I felt sick. It was disgusting. My dad's brother. I couldn't believe my mom would do that. My dad was no angel, but that was something else."

"So you decided to leave earlier than planned?" asked Ferguson.

"Right," Callie said. "I was already doing bad in school, anyway. It didn't matter, I thought." Callie had read of actors and actresses who'd made it big without high school. Education got in the way. Callie breathed heavily, hating herself. If she had only stayed in school, this would never have happened. She pictured herself staying in drama, being directed by that monster. *How naïve we all were for thinking that man was anything but terrible.*

"Are you okay, Callie?" Theresa asked. "Would you like to stop?" Callie shook her head.

"What happened with school?" Ferguson asked. "You were doing well until this last semester."

Callie lowered her head. "I just... I don't know. I was sick of it all. Mr. Greyson..." Callie could feel her blood boiling again when she thought of him. Steph was dead, but that piece of shit continued to live. "He groped Steph, okay? He did. She told me he asked her to stay after class to take a test she skipped. He said he would fail her if she didn't stay. He stood behind her as she took it. She felt his hand reach around her and grab her breast, then another one of his hands, tried to touch her. She told me what happened, and I believed her. We got to know each other in that class. You wouldn't think it, but we had things in common. I understood her. Steph told me not to tell anyone what happened with Mr. Greyson but..." Callie wiped away another tear.

"Who did you tell?" Ferguson asked in a low tone.

"Mr. Peterson," Callie answered. "I thought maybe he could do something about it."

"Did he?"

"I don't know. A friend of mine told me he wasn't coaching soccer anymore, and he stopped helping us in drama too, but he still taught! He was still teaching. He was still being a funking slimeball—Sorry."

Ferguson smiled with thin lips. "That's okay. Detective Lane and I will follow up more about that fucking slimeball soon. We're not done with him either." Callie nodded her head.

"When nothing happened," Callie continued, "I guess...it

made me sick, all of it. I started ditching more with Steph. Sometimes, Fin would pick us up from school, and we would all hang out."

"He was your boyfriend?" Ferguson asked.

"Titles never really suit a guy like Fin Lentz. He had a rep for being with a few girls at the same time."

"We interviewed a young woman named Jessica Summers," Ferguson added. "Was she one of those other girls?"

Callie nodded her head. "For a while, Jess and I were friends. Jess was seeing Fin, but they weren't really a couple. Fin would always flirt with me, but I wouldn't give him the time of day back then. I started to get to know Steph and really liked her. When I found out what Mr. Greyson had done, I told..." She paused for a moment. "I told Mr. Peterson, but I didn't realize Jess was in the auditorium. Suddenly, gossip was spreading around school that Steph Moore had slept with a teacher." Callie sighed heavily. She still felt so much anger, especially now that she knew about what happened with Steph, for what she had done. "I used to call Jess gossip queen sometimes. I never knew how ugly of a person she was until she started spreading those lies about Steph. Steph, though, she didn't want that bitch to have the upper hand. She had this blog, and she wrote about how she slept with a teacher to get a good grade. She wasn't going to let Jessica Summers dictate who she was." Callie smiled. Steph had been one of a kind. "So a little after, Fin started flirting with me, and I let it happen. I guess I liked it too. Jessica found out, and she didn't take it well." Callie lowered her head. "I made out with him in the hallways, right near her locker. I wanted her to know. I didn't want her to find out through gossip that I was hooking up with Fin. I wanted her to see it with her own eyes."

Callie hated herself in that moment. She felt sick for doing that, even though she hated Jess for what she did. Callie knew she had made a mistake when she took things too far with Fin. He was her *first*. How naïve she was that a guy like Fin would ever be more than what his nature allowed him to be. He was a sleazeball too. He slept with whatever girl he could find and then moved on to the next body.

Callie continued, "It was Fin who agreed to drive us to the bus stop in the city that day. He picked us up at the bleachers like we planned. Steph and I were already a little high." Callie smiled. "Fin was pissed, because he was supposed to get most of the weed for driving us to the bus stop. Steph climbed into the middle seat of his truck. He tried to get with Steph. I don't know, maybe in his head, he thought he could have both of us." Callie breathed in deep.

And Jessica was the one who kept calling me pig, Callie thought.

"He kicked us out of the car when Steph hit him. He left us at the school. That's where Mr. Peterson saw us. Steph opened her big mouth and asked him for a ride." She remembered how the drama teacher had looked around the empty parking lot and school premises, then he'd smiled and said he would drive them.

"Instead, he drove you right to his property?" Ferguson asked.

"No, he said he wanted to toast our send off the right way and buy some liquor. We opened a bottle of whiskey in his car after he bought a few bottles. I was out of it. We were driving in the county when I spotted my uncle's neighborhood. I begged Mr. Peterson to stop a few blocks away. I told him I had to see someone before leaving. He stopped the car, and Steph and I walked to my uncle's home. I told Steph what I wanted to do before he opened the door. He could tell we were drunk, but he saw Steph and me, and was more than willing to let us come inside. Steph flirted with him hard. I..." Callie started to feel sick again. "I flirted with him too, on purpose! When I could tell he was into it, I started laughing, and Steph joined me. We called him pitiful! Desperate. I told him I would tell my mom how sick he was. I told him my dad was going to find out too. He's scared of him." Callie lowered her head. She was scared of him. She knew if she told her dad, he would kill her uncle. "I know my uncle was a slimeball like the rest of them. He was teaching me to drive, but I caught him checking me out sometimes. It was weird, sick. I stopped asking him to teach me. When I saw him and my mom at the motel, I lost it."

Callie looked at Detective Ferguson, whose facial expression didn't change. She appreciated that, because it made her sick thinking about how she'd led on her uncle to mess with his head. She'd wanted Uncle James to know that she knew what a sick fuck he was and that the game he was playing with her, and especially her mom, was over, even if she wasn't going to be in Cranston anymore. Even on her way out of town, she was still her mother's keeper.

"You went back into Peterson's car after?" Ferguson asked.

Callie nodded her head. "He was waiting outside my uncle's house, like a getaway driver. We drove off, drinking more whiskey and laughing about what happened. Mr. Peterson said he needed to stop a few miles up the road at his house a moment. He said we could wait in the car or come out and look around. I had been to his farm before," Callie said, lowering her head. "Mr. Peterson joked about having to go to the bathroom before driving a few more hours. He had a play at his farm last semester. When we practiced there, he had this beautiful horse, Lady Laura. I said I wanted to see her again, so he brought us to the farm in the back. Steph and I petted her, fed her some hay." Callie smiled, remembering how Steph had laughed at how Lady Laura ate some of the hay from her hands. Callie lowered her head. "He asked if we had ever seen a storm shelter. He told me his father had made it but never finished it. We wanted to check it out." Callie sighed deeply.

The social worker stood up, handing a box of Kleenex to her. Callie moved the box back towards her and raised a hand. "It's okay, really. When we were down there, Steph and I were still laughing." Steph remembered how they'd kept sipping whiskey right from the bottle. Steph had grabbed a handful of clay from the unfinished walls and threw it at her, laughing hysterically. Steph had stopped laughing when she noticed the metal bars. "When we looked back at Mr. Peterson, his whole facial expression changed. He always smiled, always. But then, he just looked at us. He shoved us inside this cage and locked us in." Callie could feel her heart beating. "He tormented us for days. I had this journal on me, and he read it to me, laughing at me the whole time. He made us do things. Weird things."

The social worker looked at Detective Ferguson, who nodded. "This is going to be a tough question, Callie," she said, "but did he abuse you sexually? Did he rape you?"

Callie shook her head as she felt herself getting sick. "He could barely touch us. He would demand us to remove our bras and panties, but would never touch us. At times, he lowered his pants, but..." She could still see Steph make the mistake of laughing at him the last time she saw her. "He couldn't get erect. Steph made fun of him for it. That's when he took her out of the cell. She fought hard, but I never saw her again." Callie had been told by Detective Lane after she'd saved her what had happened to Steph. That monster had killed her. "I'm not sure how long after it was, but that's when Detective Lane found me, and you," she said, nodding her head at Detective Ferguson. Callie lowered her head. "Thank you." Callie could feel the tears forming and now falling down her cheek. She couldn't stop them now. "I was so naïve! So dumb."

Detective Ferguson handed a Kleenex to her. "Do not blame yourself for what happened. This was not the first time he did this to a young woman. This was not your fault."

Callie remembered that during the daytime, in the shelter, a streak of light would shine down, so that she could see a little. She'd seen scratch marks in the cell that weren't from Steph or her. The marks had been made by hands that were much smaller.

"One last thing," Detective Ferguson started. "Why were you wearing Steph Moore' clothes?" Callie laughed to herself. She told them how it was Steph's idea when they were waiting for Fin at the bleachers. Detective Ferguson looked at the social worker and back at Callie. "That was everything I wanted to know today. How about that ride home?"

CHAPTER THIRTY

Detective Alda Lane

One month later

Alda continued to read the news article as Ferg drove. She turned the page and looked at him with a thin smile. "Don't get used to driving," she said. "This is only temporary."

He laughed. "Sure, Alda. Doctor said at least a month of no driving because of your leg."

Alda shook her head. "Well, stop looking so happy about it." She turned the paper to the front page, smiling wider at the headline. 'Ryland Moore Released from Prison After Wrongful Conviction.' Alda had already agreed in private to give her testimony on the reasons why she didn't want to charge him murder years ago. Ryland was due for a big pay day.

Alda believed in justice, even if it was against her own side of the law. The DA's office had already called Alda in their office to get their stories straight for the pending lawsuit. Alda walked right out of their office, flipping off the DA on the way out the door. Ryland Moore would get every penny he deserved.

Ferg parked the car on the street.

"Let me do the talking, Ferg," Alda said. "You just do the driving." Ferguson nodded his head in agreement.

Alda limped her way up the walkway and onto the front porch of the Knox home. She knocked on the door loudly.

It was Callie who answered the door, opening it partway. She smiled when she saw Alda. "Detective Lane," she said. "I've been wanting to see you to thank you in person."

Alda smiled. "I wanted to thank you too," she said, looking at her leg. "You were quick on your feet, and if it weren't for you, well..."

Callie looked at Ferguson. "Thanks again." He nodded his head.

"Is your mom home?" Alda asked.

A thick hand opened the door fully. "My wife?" asked Steve Knox. "What do you want with her?"

"That would be between us, Mr. Knox," Alda said with a smile. "Is she home?"

"I told you to speak with my lawyer if you want to talk with me or my family," Steve said harshly.

"Please provide me with your lawyer's name," Alda said with a smile.

A hand went over Steve's shoulder. 'Please, Steve. It's okay," Mandy said. They spoke between themselves a moment. "I need to say it to her," Mandy said, pushing past Steve.

Mandy took a step outside on to her front porch, closing the door partly behind her. It only took a moment for Alda to smell the booze on her lips.

"How are you, Mandy?" Alda asked. "I see you and Steve are back together."

Mandy shrugged her shoulders. "Love is strange." She looked down at her porch. "Wasn't too long ago, you met me at my home that day it all started," she said. "I wanted to thank you." Mandy wiped a tear from her cheek. She suddenly stretched out her arms and hugged Alda tightly. "Thank you!" Alda let out a groan, feeling the pain from her leg. She smiled and guided Ms. Knox off of her. "Sorry!" she exclaimed. "Sorry."

"It's okay," Alda said with a smile. "I'm happy that we found Callie. That's all that mattered to me."

"Well," Mandy said with a smile, "I have to go back inside now. We're going to Steve's place. He's bringing more things to the house today."

Alda reached out and gently grabbed Mandy's shoulder.

"Sorry, Ms. Knox. One last thing." Mandy looked back at her with a solemn expression. "Do you know where James Knox is?"

Mandy looked shocked. "No. It's been over a month, and I haven't seen him."

"That's right," Detective Ferguson said. "A neighbor says a day or so before we found Callie was the last anybody saw him. He doesn't have many neighbors though. His phone records stopped showing activity the day we found Callie."

Mandy nodded her head. "Right, I'm not sure about the timeline. I was so busy with Callie, my head wasn't right." She laughed. "Look, Steve was the one who put in the missing persons case on his brother. He can tell you more, maybe."

"I highly doubt that, Ms. Knox," Detective Ferguson said. "We already talked to the detectives on James' case before coming here."

Mandy nodded her head. "Well, that's good. I hope the detectives find him."

Alda smiled. "We actually took on the case now, Ms. Knox." Mandy nodded her head. "If you tell us what happened, maybe I can help. We can talk at the station."

Steve opened the front door. "Not unless you have a warrant, you won't," he barked. He grabbed his wife's arm and harshly dragged her into the home. "Like I said, talk to my lawyer."

Alda shook her head. "I will find out what happened, Mr. Knox. I will be back."

Printed in Great Britain
by Amazon

12026562R00081